Winter's Edge

by the same author

Blood Sisters
Movement
Murder In The English Department

as co-author

Her Own Woman
Tales I Tell My Mother

Winter's Edge

Valerie Miner

METHUEN

First published in Great Britain 1984
by Methuen London Ltd
11 New Fetter Lane, London EC4P 4EE
Copyright © Valerie Miner 1984
Set in IBM 11 point Journal by 𝒜 Tek-Art, Croydon, Surrey
Printed and bound in Great Britain
by Redwood Burn Ltd., Trowbridge, Wiltshire

ISBN 0 413 53920 2 (hardback)
ISBN 0 413 53930 X (paperback)

For my mother,
Mary Gill McKenzie Miner

Acknowledgements

Writing is for me a social act at the beginning and at the end. I think fiction emerges from an imaginative collectivity of writers and readers rather than from solitary genesis. Stimulus for this novel as well as motivation for the novelist came from many people. I would like to name a few who have been particularly helpful over the years.

Winter's Edge is dedicated to Mary Miner with gratitude for her love, optimism and original wit.

Three friends have read almost every word of my rough drafts. For their persistent criticism and support. I heartily thank Deborah Johnson, Eve Pell and Peggy Webb.

Many people have read this manuscript and/or given me technical advice. I owe much to Sandy Boucher, Kim Chernin, Sara Colm, Susan Griffin, Marlene Griffith, Jana Harris, Carol Kotewicz, Joyce Lindenbaum, Mary Mackey, Debbie Matsumoto, Cathy Merschel, Betty Medsger, Raul Ramirez, Betty Roszak, Eleanor Scully, Barbara Wilson and the reference staff of the Berkeley Public Library.

For her sensitive editorial counsel, I acknowledge Elsbeth Lindner. For her good sense, bright spirit and patient encouragement, I thank Helen Longino.

Winter's Edge takes place in an imaginary café and an imaginary news shop on an imaginary corner of San Francisco. Even the electoral district has been gerrymandered. However, since readers always hunt for ghosts, it's worth adding the old refrain, 'This book is a work of fiction and any resemblance to persons, living or dead, is coincidental.'

One

'Warn me never to order Mummer's "mystery meat" again,' groaned Chrissie as she marched ahead of her old friend.

'I reminded you this time.' Margaret deliberately maintained her slower pace. It had taken ten minutes to persuade Chrissie into a stroll and now she was moving like one of those marathon joggers, as if covering ground were the whole point of human existence. Tightly, Margaret held Slocum's leash, because the dog preferred Chrissie's clip.

Annoyed with Margaret's dainty steps, then annoyed with herself for forgetting Margaret's varicose veins, then annoyed with those lame legs as further evidence that Margaret Sawyer had hardly received a fair deal these seventy years, Chrissie emitted a gutteral, 'Och!' Because she couldn't complain about Margaret's not complaining, she returned to the foul dinner.

'Aye, you told me, but Gudrun insisted it was tasty tonight. We Scots have always known the Swedes were barbarians. Urrrrph,' she burped, 'I wouldn't be surprised if what I ate was minced...' she paused, bent down and whispered the last word in Slocum's floppy ear, 'dog!'

Slocum jumped against Chrissie's wool skirt, excitement rippling the golden fur along her back.

'Chrissie MacInnes, you're a hopeless tease.' Margaret was caught between fondness and irritation, familiar territory with Chrissie. Soon Slocum calmed down and Chrissie wound up. She didn't stop chattering all the way back to Geary Street.

'Marissa Washington will be the best supervisor San Francisco ever had,' Chrissie declared. 'She'll blast out those bloody developers.'

'Reverend Bentman says we need more business to support the downtown community.'

'Don't tell me your passion for the parson has knocked all the sense from your head.'

Margaret was speechless. She liked Reverend Bentman. Admired was a more appropriate term.

'Marissa will revitalize the Tenderloin,' Chrissie persisted. 'We'll be well represented by a sharp black woman who . . .'

Margaret tuned out. She wouldn't bother to respond as Chrissie held forth. She was such an unassailable personality with these long strides, her gunmetal grey head high in the air. Did Chrissie notice the thin lady over there in the yellowing lace dress? Cotton and lace in autumn. Margaret shivered. Did Chrissie see how young this worn-out prostitute was? Of course, Chrissie understood it all, Margaret reconsidered, far better than she herself did. Chrissie understood how and why the neighborhood did and didn't fit together — all these different races and political groups and down-and-outers and ambitious immigrants. She had told Margaret how some of her friends over on Eddy Street considered Geary quite posh.

Chrissie waved to Hank at Risco Liquors. She noticed little Pete selling his pencils near the alley. And a drunk at the tavern door pretending to play blue grass on a splintered broomstick. Of course, Margaret thought, Chrissie saw everything. She saw *well beyond* everything.

As they neared Mummer's Café, Slocum started barking again. Margaret was surprised at the dog's nervousness, since she often wandered this block alone. She bent down to calm her.

Chrissie heard the men first. 'Step back, Margaret,' she ordered.

They moved against the beige brick building to avoid three pale young men running along the sidewalk. Chrissie peered after the details: white, early twenties, good clothes. She didn't recognize any of them.

Slocum began to howl, hearing the siren before the women did.

Chrissie clenched her fists. The sound of cops always set her on edge. Trouble here, they warned: change lanes; cross the street; avert your eyes. Irrational reaction, she knew. Police usually arrived after the trouble began, like blisters on a burn. Still, the sirens bloated her with fear.

Margaret turned and started briskly toward their apartment building. Chrissie was headed in the direction of the sirens.

2

'Come on, Margaret. We're safe now. Trouble's gone that way,' she pointed after the young men.

Margaret supposed she was right. Since she didn't relish walking home alone, she followed Chrissie, keeping her own gait and holding Slocum close.

By the time they reached the corner, the crowd was already passing rumors, 'Mugged him coming out of the alley there.' 'Looks like a broken arm.' 'Ah, come on, it's all right. He'll live.'

Chrissie grabbed Margaret's hand, yanking her to the front of the spectators. Two white policemen were bent over a middle-aged black man. One of the officers seemed to be calling an ambulance on his radio.

'Harold!' exclaimed Chrissie. She turned to Margaret, 'It's Harold Lawson, Marissa's campaign manager.' Margaret nodded dumbly. Chrissie dropped her hand and hurried over to Lawson.

So like Chrissie, Margaret considered, to be acquainted with the centre of attention. Margaret felt like she didn't know a soul. She didn't want to. She simply wanted to be back in her apartment, resting against a friendly pillow. She stared at the puddles, blinking back neon signs. The sidewalk along Geary Street still shone slick from the late afternoon shower. People rushed past each other, as if under shell fire. The puddles pulsated blue and red. Blood red. This was not Vietnam; she felt a stab about her son Michael. This was San Francisco in 1979. No soldiers here. Margaret's thoughts were interrupted by voices, so many loud voices. Across the crowd, someone was nodding to her.

Margaret squinted, recognized Reverend Bentman and blushed. He smiled in a neighborly way. She responded like-wise, wondering about her initial girlish response.

'We'll get them, Harold,' Chrissie promised. 'When Marissa's elected, we'll get all of them.' An ambulance siren cut through the night, drowning Chrissie's voice.

Margaret noticed Harold Lawson's jaw relax, whether because of the ambulance's arrival or Chrissie's departure, she couldn't tell. Everyone watched silently as they eased the shivering man on to a stretcher and then into the blinking vehicle.

3

Chrissie took full advantage of the crowd. 'Harold will be okay. His arm will heal. The question is will the Tenderloin survive? Without an honest . . .'

'So's your old lady,' heckled a man, sipping from a bottle in a brown paper bag.

'Right on, Chrissie,' said a dark woman near the front of the crowd.

Margaret didn't know what got into her, but she grabbed Chrissie's arm and drew her along the sidewalk. 'Time to go home. The election isn't until November.'

'If we last that long,' Chrissie rasped. 'This brutality! This violence!'

Slocum, held tight on the leash, pulled Margaret who was pulling Chrissie. As they passed the spot where the three young men had shot by, the dog began to whine.

Two

That September, no one could have predicted the extent of violence to follow. However, Chrissie insisted Harold Lawson's broken arm was a campaign casualty. She didn't let a day pass without coming into the news shop where Margaret worked and arguing politics.

Sometimes Margaret looked at Chrissie and pretended her friend wasn't talking. Margaret blotted out the words and watched the strong face she had known for three decades. She observed the tension in Chrissie's powerful shoulders and the flapping of her large hands; she counted the grey curls under Chrissie's taut hair net. Sometimes Margaret waded into the deep blue eyes and rested in their friendship. Such reverie never lasted long. Chrissie's tart brogue always pierced Margaret back to attention. Chrissie had learned to tell when Margaret had tuned out.

'The election is vital to all of us,' Chrissie was instructing, preaching. She regarded Margaret, poised behind the cash register. Poised. Margaret was so damn poised, so conscious of deportment. Posture perfect, as if Mother had balanced a book on her head. She was a good woman, a decent woman, but so *damn* well-behaved.

'Marissa Washington is fighting for all of us who live in downtown San Francisco,' Chrissie resumed. 'Blacks, whites, poor old women like us.'

Margaret shook her head, willing Chrissie to lower her voice. She straightened the fresh pile of *San Francisco Chronicle*s and looked around to determine whether anyone were listening. Old woman indeed. How old could she look with her black, straight hair, newly hennaed yesterday? All right for Chrissie to identify with Senior Citizens. But Margaret Sawyer was no fool. She didn't want to be old. She knew the line between respect and sympathy.

'Seven-thirty in the morning,' Chrissie persisted loudly.

'Seven-thirty in the morning and you'll work in this news shop until what time?'

Would Chrissie get worse as the campaign continued, Margaret wondered. This was only September, for heaven's sake.

Slocum barked, balancing her front paws on the counter, her watery eyes gazing playfully at Chrissie. Margaret raised her right brow, a familiar signal that she had had enough. She pushed Slocum beneath the counter and pulled out a chartreuse feather duster, whisking around the cigarette case and over the packages of sugarless gum. All right for Chrissie to claim old age. But Margaret knew that she, herself, looked sixty, maybe fifty-five. Dr Branson had said that, completely unsolicited, at the last check-up. So she got away with it. Got away with putting ten years less on her forms. Got away with indigo hair at age seventy. Got away with working from early morning until after dark. The store was her life. What would she do without it?

'It's a split shift,' she whispered to Chrissie, still hoping she would lower her volume.

'Split shift, my arse,' said Chrissie. 'Marissa says it's liberals — and Douglas is a liberal of the highest sort — who commit the worst labor infractions. You need a union.'

Margaret moved her stockinged feet deeper in Slocum's thick, warm fur. The dog sighed contentedly and rolled back against her stool. Margaret knew not to provoke Chrissie further. She didn't want an argument to carry back to the room where her boss, Douglas Sinclair, was watching *Good Morning America.*

Still, Margaret couldn't help herself. She answered in a sharp, hot voice, 'I suppose the union is what got you dolled up in that outfit? Chrissie MacInnes, sixty-five-year old firebomb, dressed in her Mummer's Café uniform, pink striped dress, revealing aging but supple knees. And those ruffles around the collar!'

'Excuse me,' Officer Hunter interrupted gently.

'Yes, sir,' said Margaret, accepting twenty cents for *The Chronicle.* The young, blond policeman was one of Margaret's favorites. Besides, it did no harm to be friendly with the police. Everyone knew that.

Hunter tipped his hat and Margaret smiled. She had good rapport with customers. Douglas Sinclair was always complimenting her on it. But then, she enjoyed working with the public.

Emboldened by her success, she turned back to Chrissie. 'You looking to get me fired with your loud voice?'

'Blah,' laughed Chrissie. 'Dougie boy ain't never going to fire you. More likely he'll marry you.'

'Enough, Chrissie.' Margaret spoke fast to keep Chrissie from noticing her blush. 'Don't you think you better get over to Mummer's or does the union also protect you from being late?'

Two men in dark suits walked into the shop. Margaret called good morning to the tall one, young Kevin Sinclair. His companion's face was shadowed beneath a large brown hat. They walked to the back of the store, then up the stairs to Kevin's real estate office.

'Crikey, you're right.' Chrissie checked her watch. 'Off I go to another morning of Sunrise Omelettes and Cable Car Waffles.' She blew her friend a kiss, rushing out the door. Thirty seconds later she returned. 'Almost forgot.' She handed Margaret two dimes for *The Chronicle*. 'See you for Scrabble tomorrow?'

'Yes, my place, tomorrow.' Margaret watched fondly as her friend left again.

Feeling guilty for chatting so long with Chrissie, she straightened the piles of *New York Times, Los Angeles Times, San Francisco Chronicles* which she had carefully arranged fifteen minutes before. She shared Douglas Sinclair's pride in the shop. Sometimes it seemed more of a library than a store because people browsed for hours. Sinclair loved being summoned from the back office for consultation about an obscure magazine or a political debate. He filled the shop with music from his classical collection, which was particularly rich in violin concertos. The music Margaret could do without, but it was *his* shop.

Stroking Slocum's fur with her toes, she considered what Chrissie had said about their equal relationship: Margaret's food for Slocum's warmth. What would she do without Chrissie? The real question was what would she do *with*

Chrissie? Now she feared that Chrissie would want to put a Marissa Washington poster in the shop window. Would Sinclair go for that? What would she do without this job?

Often it felt like family here — Douglas Sinclair telling his droll stories about the old-time Tenderloin, about the Roaring Twenties' speakeasies, about Al Jolson at the Barbary Coast. She liked Kevin just as much, although father and son didn't get along. Kevin Sinclair was always remembering her with a bit of candy or a flower or a book before he went upstairs to his office. Such a decent, up-and-coming young man he was. Why the tension with his father? Well, family fights were normal and this one was none of her business.

Margaret did wish her own children lived close. Not that she wanted pampering, but she'd like to see their faces once in a while. She glanced at the three photographs next to the cigarette price sheet. Michael, shot in some Vietnam swamp. Poor Michael, nineteen, killed during his first week at the DMZ, ten years before. No one ever talked about that war. No one remembered Michael, really. His brother and sister, maybe — but Rob was off fishing in Alaska and Janey, beautiful Janey, was writing poetry in the wilds of British Columbia. Margaret Sawyer's daughter, a famous poet. She had been proud to show Janey's photograph to Mr Sinclair that day she made it to page twenty-six of *Time* Magazine. Janey Sawyer kept her family name, unlike some of those stars. Of course she wasn't really a star. She was a good daughter. She wrote letters every couple of weeks. The girl deserved a life of her own. Margaret knew that she was luckier than most mothers.

'Morning Maggie, *mi amiga.*' Roberto wheeled his cart into the store. He talked rapidly as he loaded papers for his news stand down the street. 'Cold enough for you?'

Slocum whined — such a flirt that dog — until Roberto reached over and scratched behind her ears. Roberto, a short, swarthy man in his mid-thirties, was popular with them both.

'Ah, don't tease.' Margaret pulled the blanket around her knees. 'Close the door and come in properly.'

'Yes, mam,' he mocked her. '*Diablo*, that wind's frozen today.'

'Yes,' shivered Margaret, 'goes straight to the bones. But

then we're lucky not to be back in New York where I grew up.'

'Only gringoes would place the soul of their country in a frozen land like New York or Washington. Now, in Mexico, September is a beautiful month, with bougainvillea streaming over the houses. When are you going to visit my country, Mama?' he smiled, knowing the answer by heart.

'Roberto, don't call me Mama,' she said, aligning her spine and moving her head so that the fluorescent light might catch the deep blues in her hair. 'Call me *amiga* or *hermana*.' She was pleased with the new words he had taught her. 'And I'll go to your charming country when . . .'

He joined her, 'When one of the Rockefellers dies and leaves me a fortune.'

They laughed together.

'So why did you come in this morning except to freeze off my toes with that wind, insult me and invite me to your long, lost rancho?'

'To ask if you want some coffee on my way back from Mummer's' he said, feigning hurt feelings.

'Oh, now, wouldn't that be nice,' she smiled as she reached into her purse. 'Why yes, don't mind if I do. With just a drop of milk and half a teaspoon of sugar?'

She offered him fifty cents, but he shook his head. 'At your service.' He was gone before she could protest.

Margaret looked out the window as her friend dodged the traffic and ran into Mummer's. Occasionally she did believe that they lived in a 'downtown community' as Reverend Bentman said. And this was how she described it to Janey in answer to that last, worried letter. It was a fine life, being near friends who took care of each other, and serving customers (some of them quite famous and prestigious) who knew her by name and remembered her at Christmas. Things could be a lot worse. She could be cooped up in one of those suburban senior citizen residences like her friend Lenore. All very well to have your room and board subsidized, with free bus excursions on Wednesdays and with Saturday social evenings. But how could anyone live off in Daly City like that? Lenore might as well be in Yokahama for the amount they saw of each other. No thank you, Margaret preferred her independence and her downtown life, even if she had to work split shift for it.

Downtown was really the end of the Theatre District or the beginning of the Tenderloin, depending on your mood. Porn shops and fur emporia. Tourists from Milwaukee and slinky hookers from The Road Runner Bar. Doormen at fancy hotels stuffing bribes from cabbies inside their handsome white gloves. Covert customers ducking in and out of Les Nuits de Paris Massage Parlor.

Geary Street, between the Theatre District and the deeper Tenderloin, was as well lit as any border, thought Margaret. Blinking red lights. White neon, smothering the neighborhood like an electric layer of tension, day and night. After dark everything seemed brighter and louder. Flashes of headlamp. Twirling red, white and blue sirens. Fluorescent vigils in the stores — advertising goods to window shoppers and second-guessing nocturnal thieves. Distant lights from Twin Peaks and Nob Hill. So distant that on black nights it was hard to distinguish them from benevolent stars. And the downtown lights were amplified by downtown noises. Honking horns. Alarm bells. Friends shouting to friends. Drivers cursing out their car windows. Children bawling.

Most of the Tenderloin kids, it seemed, were from the new Indo-Chinese families who lived blocks away. So Margaret did hear young voices occasionally. Until the children grew mute in this concrete country. Awed by the tall greyness of it all, overwhelmed by the size of once great hotels and wheezing buses. Silenced by anticipation. Yes, in this never-never land, things happened. Erupted. A few streets toward Union Square, Broadway plays were produced. And just yesterday, several blocks in the other direction, over on Turk Street, a policeman from Harlem was shot to death. On vacation from one of America's worst slums and he was shot to death in San Francisco. Margaret shook her head. Terrible. Of course it was terrible. But the underlying question, the part she couldn't understand, was why he was walking there at three am.

Actually, she did walk that part of Turk herself, but only in broad daylight, with Slocum on a short leash. She walked there maybe once a week to shop at the cut-rate drugstore or to visit Gudrun. But she always kept to the edge of the sidewalk, alert so she could run into the traffic if she needed to escape. Dreadful state of affairs, Chrissie would complain to her. What kind of world was it where you were safer to risk being run over than talking to somebody? Chrissie, too, was adept at dodging those people.

'Those people.' People, yes, but strange, thought Margaret. Not our type. Thin from drink and smoke. Pale faces on birdlike bodies. Bleached blond hair and fake leopard coats. Walking through the city as if numb to street lights and honking horns. Only a couple of years ago Margaret had noticed how many of *those* people were younger than herself. Somehow she had classified down-and-outers as folk from another era. A former era. But here they were, some of them forty, fifty years *younger.* All of them moving blindly and deafly through the city. People of an ageless tribe. Hunters and gatherers in the garbage bins and open handbags. Defiant, cold, hard beyond the luxury of anger. Of course, some of them were ingenious in their survival. But others seemed to continue because they were too stupid or too tired or too bitter to die. The Tenderloin. Some people eat well, Chrissie would say, but everyone starves in one sense or another.

Three

Mummer's was busy that morning. During the first forty-five minutes, Chrissie served pounds of Sunrise Omlettes, Cable Car Waffles and home fries. The people at Table 11 wanted a little cider vinegar, if she didn't mind. Australians. They were getting more and more of these tourists now that Mr M had plugged into the bus packages. Cider vinegar; she smiled, remembering Edinburgh. The best part of Saturday night at the cinema was the aroma of fish and chips soaked in enough vinegar to carry you home through the bitter chill.

One of those mornings, all right. 'Que Sera Sera', 'Paperback Writer', 'Blue Velvet' on the whining muzak. Eight-thirty before she could lean against the window frame and stare out at the early autumn smog. San Francisco was getting as bad as LA. Across the street, she could see Margaret busy with her feather mop. Probably doing the third dust of Douglas Sinclair's impulse items today. That woman was exasperating with her notions of duty and diplomacy. She felt 'privileged' to work for Douglas because she was fond of the shop and of the folks who passed through. Nothing wrong with that, Chrissie thought. She also enjoyed her job, but she wasn't going to suffer for it. You had a right to work *and* a right to be treated fairly. Margaret said Douglas was like family. Sure, the bossy father. He exploited . . . no, she, couldn't use such language with Margaret. Her friend insisted on seeing everything as personal, as something to be worked out between one individual and another. Margaret didn't believe she was part of a world that contained more than two people at a time.

'So who are you arguing with now?' came a low, unmistakeably Swedish voice.

Chrissie turned to Gudrun, grinning. 'Was my face that obvious?'

'*Ja*, well, there was enough of a glower that we had to turn up the lights a few notches,' the other waitress laughed.

12

Chrissie regarded Gudrun with affectionate curiosity. She was a tall woman in her early fifties with pretty Nordic features and platinum blond hair. Gudrun carried her large, rounded body gracefully, owning every ounce as a source of potential energy. She was a softie like Margaret, however she also had a practical side. That included her 'evening companion work'.

Gudrun was smart about it; she wouldn't get consumed. Chrissie knew a lot of prostitutes, women who did tricks all night. But they usually lasted only a year or two in the Tenderloin before they invested too much of their wages directly into their veins or else they moved on. If that could be called moving. Gudrun had kept the work part-time and had lasted ten years at it. Usually this aspect of her life was unapparent unless she came in with bruises or bags under her eyes. Gudrun must have taken last night off because she looked rested this morning. And maybe a little too sassy.

Chrissie surfaced. 'Oh, I was just talking with Margaret about the elections.'

'A sure bet for argument,' Gudrun said. 'Still, you both thrive on fighting.'

'Hmmm.' Chrissie felt the depth of her frustration with Margaret. 'How can a developer's clown like Jake Carson do that well in the polls?'

'I was listening to the phone-ins last night,' Gudrun said. 'The callers didn't think Carson was a joke.'

'Phone-ins!' exclaimed Chrissie. 'Is that your idea of political discussion? They're about the same level as soap opera.'

'Snob,' laughed Gudrun. 'Phone-ins are people's politics, public forums, *you* should approve. Anyway, everyone is afraid of depression. They think Carson's going to bring jobs and money.'

'Money!' Chrissie erupted, then looked around to make sure they weren't being overheard and that there were no new customers at her station. She'd have to refill the coffee on Table 12 in a minute, but she had time to set Gudrun straight. 'Money for whom? Carson will just bring in more hotels. Who profits from that? The Hilton grosses 1.6 million a year. Don't kid yourself. We won't even get a raise of fifty cents an hour.'

Gudrun tugged at the back of her maroon cap, rearranging the clear plastic bobby pins which gave it the illusion of floating on her blonde curls. Chrissie, who had steadfastly refused the cap and had won a union battle over it (damned if she were going to turn into Shirley Temple forty years too late) was intrigued by the way Gudrun wore the silly thing, with such seeming effortlessness. Gudrun, she considered, was one of those women who worked very hard at making things appear effortless. Her turquoise earrings nodded gently between her bright curls. She always managed a touch of blue.

'And what's more,' Chrissie continued, 'Carson can't be declaring all the campaign contributions.'

Gudrun stepped back and stared critically. 'You be careful, Ms MacInnes.'

'Och,' Chrissie waved Gudrun away as she walked toward the Silex station for the coffee pot.

'Some nice hot coffee?' she inquired at Table 12. Then to the Australians at Table 11. She waved to Roberto who was carrying a couple of 'to go' coffees. She nodded to Mr Poulos as he slipped in the side door and sat at Table 15, by the window. Poulos stared across Geary Street as if he were planning to scale one of the seven-storey buildings. Chrissie followed his gaze down the beige, mustard, grey and brown façades. Since his family had owned the drugstore here for three generations, he took a certain weatherbeaten pride in the street. A 38 Geary bus pulled in front of a Gallo delivery truck setting off a cacophony of horns and brake squeals. Poulos looked at his newspaper.

Every morning at eight-forty-five, Poulos sat down at Table 15. Jeannette, the cashier, knew not to seat anyone else there, even when it was crowded like this morning. And Chrissie knew to bring Mr Poulos his orange juice first, then the coffee in ten minutes. Some mornings they didn't exchange two words. She watched Poulos lean back against the maroon booth in his grey tweed suit, a deep rich grey. Chrissie had noticed that the fastidious druggist had stopped wearing the green gaberdine after Mr M had changed the café décor (and the waitresses' uniforms which were, no doubt, part of the décor) from brown tones to maroon, pink and white. Peppermint-stick cute. She had tried to complain through the

14

union that they deserved some say in the color scheme — that it was all part of their working conditions — but she had won only the right to be capless.

Mr Poulos glanced up from *The Chronicle* as Chrissie served his orange juice. 'Now here's a man who's going to restore prosperity to the neighborhood.' He tapped Carson's grey and white photograph with his spoon.

Chrissie knew that she shouldn't let him goad her, however it was too much for one morning: Margaret, Gudrun and now Poulos.

'Prosperity,' she exploded, as one used to sputtering in small spaces. 'Prosperity for a few absentee landlords, and disaster for the people who *live* in this neighborhood. Have you seen those "senior hotels"? Faulty wiring, garbage piling in the hallways, elevators broken for six months. Prosperity! Come on, tell me more, tell me how, who?'

'Smoggy day.' He stared out to Geary Street.

Again she followed his gaze across the traffic, to the façade of Sinclair's News, the faded italic logo next to the bright red sign of the Verygood Butchershop. On the other side was the blue-painted entry to the apartment house where she and Margaret lived. Near the door was a plaque honoring Alicia Goldman, 'noted radical and artist, who lived here from 1910-1920'.

'They'll have a plaque for you one day soon,' Poulos smiled, revived by his orange juice.

'Don't rush me to the grave.' Chrissie swivelled at the bell indicating the hot chocolate was ready for Table 11.

'The farthest thing from my mind,' chuckled Poulos tipping an imaginary hat.

'I'm sure it was,' she laughed back. Chrissie wondered if the reason she liked Poulos, despite all their differences, was that he could take a good tease.

The hot chocolate was a success with the Australian lad, whose eyes lit up at the extra inch of whipped cream Chrissie had lavished in his cup.

She leaned against a wall by the kitchen until it was time for Poulos's coffee. Fatigue would take her at odd moments like this. She wished she could sleep more, could get back into her old habit of ten hours a night. Yet as she grew older, it was hard to sleep in the mornings. Maybe the body's timer was saying, 'You're closing in. Take as many hours as you can.' Death was a curious shadow, a kind of companionable silhouette nowadays rather than the dark pathway she imagined as a girl. When she was younger, she would stare at old people and feel melancholy, thinking how sad that life was almost over for them. Now sometimes she looked at young folks and felt great sympathy for all the miles ahead. She didn't want to die. Doubtless, she would leave fighting, but she no longer felt any panic about her own death. Occasionally she regarded the notion with a certain serenity.

Suddenly aware of an itch on her neck, she brushed away a plastic leaf drooping from the pink trellis. Often she felt she worked in a dolls' house because of these plastic plants and the ceiling fans rotating in languid uselessness and the fake gas lanterns above the bricked-up fireplace. She didn't understand such taste. It was so obviously artificial. Did the customers pretend the vinyl tablecloths were linen and the muzak tunes were intelligible? Did they find the imitation-imitation cute? Sometimes she thought that Americans suffered from a massively short-circuited imagination.

Poulos, engrossed in the sports page, accepted his coffee with a silent nod.

She walked over to Gudrun who was standing at the window, hands on hips, watching Ernie saunter out of Sinclair's News.

'You've got to be kidding, Gerdie, with this crush on Ernie. Gay men don't convert.'

'Maybe.' Gudrun smiled from some inner wisdom. 'We'll see. Anyway, why are you so worried about my "crush"?'

'Just hate to see you hopping after a man. Like Margaret. You both believe in security. But nothing's secure — lovers, kids, even friends.'

Gudrun watched Chrissie with exaggerated patience, as if waiting for her top to spin down.

'The only reliability in the world is yourself,' Chrissie said. 'And unless you contribute, even that disappears.'

'Why so philosophical this morning?' Gudrun tipped her head to an almost ninety degree angle, the tiny maroon cap remaining absolutely still. Chrissie noticed that Gudrun's cap, as well as her hair, was heavily lacquered and wondered if you could get cancer from hair spray.

'Och, you know me.' Chrissie was suddenly self-conscious. 'I wouldn't be happy if I weren't complaining and offering advice. It's my "tight little Scottish personality", as I believe you called it last week.'

'Ohhhh,' said Gudrun, 'I thought you liked teasing.'

'Must be getting soft.'

'Chrissie MacInnes, you've always been soft. You're only a tight-ass Scot when it comes to romance. Otherwise you are generous to a fault.'

'Fault? Me? The very idea.'

'Seriously, why don't you fall in love? Why don't you want a man in your life?'

'I had enough men in my life — until I was twenty, six brothers. And if they taught me one thing, it was that I didn't need to spend my time having men need me.'

'Something missing from this story.' Gudrun shook her head slowly.

'Speaking of stories,' Chrissie sobered abruptly, 'did you read yesterday's article on Tenderloin Characters? Would they print an article about Pacific Heights Characters? Even when they're trying to be sympathetic they make this place out to be a carnival. Really, do you *know* any Tenderloin characters?'

They both looked up as Mr Poulos waved for a coffee refill. Chrissie reached over to the Silex pot. Gudrun spoke under her breath, 'I know one character.'

Chrissie turned to retort and spotted a figure entering the cafe: Marissa Washington, her arms loaded with manilla envelopes. Chrissie forgot her rebuttal and hurried to Poulos's table.

She tried to catch Marissa's eye, but the large black woman had seated herself on the waiting couch near the cash register and was busily working on something. Never wasted a minute, Marissa, that was one of her most admirable and irritating qualities. Marissa had quantities of energy set to constructive purposes. If Margaret thought Chrissie was busy, she should meet Marissa. Now, every inch of her was assigned to the current task, her thin brows furrowed, her broad mauve

17

mouth pursed, one hand gripping the envelopes, the other dashing a pencil across the page.

Then, as Chrissie approached, Marissa smiled, stood and shifted her papers. The big woman caressed Chrissie with her one free arm, kissing her quickly on the cheek. With surprise, Chrissie noticed she was as tall as her friend. She returned the kiss and stepped back stiffly.

'Can't stay a second.' Marissa leafed through her envelopes. 'But Harold was supposed to bring you the mailing list and he got sidetracked.'

'Marissa, you're too busy for this sort of clerical task.'

'Since when do you believe in hierarchies?' the other woman chided. She glanced at her watch and shook her head as if to clear her mind. 'Got to go. Already five minutes late for a meeting.'

'Aye,' said Chrissie. 'I'll get those flyers off tonight.'

'Bye angel,' Marissa waved as she rushed out.

The café door swung lazily after her, admitting the rat-rat-rat of a drill from the sidewalk. Chrissie paused by the window to observe Marissa's progress up Geary Street toward Jones. Marissa waved at a burly Chinese man who had double-parked in front of the liquor shop. His arms full of La Batts beer, he nodded back. Horns sounded behind him which he stalwartly ignored, lugging the cases over the sidewalk and into the store. Chrissie considered how every inch of the city was reserved. Parking spaces in blue, yellow, white, grey were marked by different-priced meters. In the lots, you could pay five to ten dollars an hour just to park six feet of car. You had to stay alert in the city. You had to know what you wanted, how long it would take. Concentration. Everything was concentrated. People advertised on the tops of cabs, the sides of buses, billboards, magazine racks. Men inched along scaffolding above the street. Every window indicated more people working or sleeping or eating. Why, there were thousands of windows on this block alone. Marissa was almost at the corner. She had stopped to talk with a Vietnamese family, moving her parcels to her left arm, so she could point them in the right direction.

Four

'Morning Mrs Sawyer.' The man's voice roused her.

Margaret turned from the window and sat straighter on her stool. She was startled, then embarrassed, to find Kevin Sinclair beaming at her. He must have tiptoed down from his office. Yes, tall, ruddy Kevin and the smaller man under the hat.

'Did I wake you?' he frowned.

'Oh, yes. I mean, no.' She tried to compose herself. Was he teasing or scolding? She knew that he liked her. Heavens, she had worked in his father's shop since he was a teenager. But he would be the boss one day. With manhood comes, well, a certain distance. She regarded him more closely. No, he was smiling. He must have been teasing. And he was holding something behind his back.

'Gardenia.' He laughed at how his manner had fooled her. 'One look at this gardenia and I said, "That belongs to Margaret."'

She wondered why other people didn't see the bright side of Kevin. Douglas Sinclair was always complaining that Kevin was ineffectual; Chrissie said he was a phoney. They just didn't understand that his caution came from a tender nature. His main fault, as far as she could tell, was his nervousness. Even that was disappearing as he became more involved in his downtown development work.

'Lovely flower,' she said. 'You shouldn't have.'

He brushed aside her thanks. 'Have you met Jake Carson?'

Carson gripped her hand tightly.

Margaret tried not to be obvious as she withdrew her hand and rubbed the finger which his ring had squashed. He was smiling rather at lot, but she supposed that politicians always wore that overly sugared disposition.

'Jake Carson,' Kevin repeated, 'our next district supervisor.'

'Pleased to meet you, sir,' said Margaret, finally recalling where she had seen the face. (On television last night. Chrissie had dropped by to watch the news and they hadn't stopped arguing all evening.) 'I wish you luck with your campaign.'

'Luck?' Kevin shook his head. 'Luck has nothing to do with it. He's the voice of reason and progress, right, Jake?'

Carson nodded amiably and then cleared his throat.

'Enough chitchat,' Kevin declared. 'Tell Dad I've gone out for a few hours, if you see him.'

'Right,' Margaret nodded. 'Thanks again for the lovely flower.'

Such a sweet boy, Kevin. Something about him reminded her of Michael. Margaret was relieved when he finally found his niche in this real estate business. He had been floundering for years. Douglas Sinclair was always so worried, and a little harsh on him, if anyone asked her, but no one did and she knew enough to keep out of it. So Kevin wasn't the brightest mind, so he hadn't become a lawyer or a professor as Sinclair had hoped. You can't design your children. At least he had the comfort of the boy living nearby — of working just upstairs, for God's sake. And Kevin seemed to be faring better lately. Well enough to buy himself an LTD. Green velvet upholstery and pushbutton windows. It wasn't everyone's employer's son who would take her out for a birthday drive in his new car to Half Moon Bay. Chrissie said he was spoiled. But then Chrissie specialized in complaints.

Margaret studied the flower. Kevin was always, once or twice a month, bringing her flowers from those pretty little stands on Powell Street. And she had never had the heart to tell him that she was allergic to them — well, not exactly allergic, but they did bother her sinus Godalmighty. She would wear them until the end of the day and give them to Chrissie, or if Chrissie were in a bad mood — and she could gripe about anything, that woman — Margaret would give the flowers to old Mrs Winchester down the hall, who was just the opposite of Chrissie, too desperate for a kind word. This way everyone was happy: Mrs Winchester, herself, Kevin.

Roberto dashed in just long enough to drop off the coffee, scratch Slocum's nose and wave to Margaret. '*Hasta pronto,* Mama.'

Surprisingly quiet for this time of morning, Margaret

20

thought as she sipped the sweet brown liquid, enjoying the slow passage of warmth through her chilled body. She remembered Chrissie protesting how Douglas Sinclair could afford a space heater. She preferred Slocum to a space heater. Digging her toes into the dog's fur, she recalled the day Janey gave her Slocum. That was almost ten years ago now, before she left for Canada. Margaret looked at the photo of her daughter on the wall: Janey smiling in front of a Vancouver Island cabin. Janey had always won her way.

Margaret had hated dogs. A waste of time. Besides, she was allergic to pollen and fur, Dr Branson told her.

'That's just psychological,' Janey had said. 'A single woman in the city needs protection,' she softened, 'as well as good company.'

'I can't possibly,' Margaret began, wondering how her own daughter — aged twenty, a woman for the last what? two or three years — was teaching her about the needs of 'a woman in the city'.

'Sure you can, Mom, give it a try. She's a good pup. I've had her spayed. She'll grow big and —'

'And eat me out of house and home.'

'Oh, Mom, you like feeding lost souls. Besides, what will you do with the three of us off your hands? Rob fishing for gold in Alaska, me exiled in Canada and Michael off . . .'

Janey couldn't bear to admit her brother would go to Vietnam that fall. It was hard for any of them to talk about it.

'You'll love her. I promise,' laughed Janey. 'Just watch. Come on, pup. Come on. Come.'

The dog advanced gingerly, as if the women might bite. Margaret was touched by her discombobulated gait.

'She's slow,' said Janey.

'She just needs a name,' Margeret took over. 'Nobody answers to "pup".'

Delighted by her mother's interest and exasperated with the dog, Janey stood back, her arms firm across her chest.

'Come, Slow,' Janey teased.

The dog held still.

'How about Slow, Come,' laughed Margaret. The puppy ran to the smiling woman, jumped up and licked her face.

'Slocum,' Margaret gasped as the dog continued jumping.

Two days passed before Margaret realized she hadn't sneezed. Perhaps she wasn't allergic to this particular animal.

'Good morning to you.'

Another voice broke through her thoughts. Lord, she was behaving like an old woman today.

'Good morning to you. Good morning, dear Margaret. Good morning to you.'

She didn't need to turn around. Ernie. Was it that late? Ernie's visit already. She had better sharpen up. Work would be hectic until eleven-thirty, the wind whipping in on the end of every friendly voice. ('Morning Margaret.' 'Hello there, Ernie . . . Mrs Dougal . . . Captain George . . . Reverend Bentman . . . Harvey . . . Little Pete.')

'Morning, Ernie.' Margaret rolled up copies of *The Chronicle* and *The New York Times.* He liked to scan the papers while waiting for customers at his flower stand on Mason Street. The smart ones always read *The Times.* She liked it herself, when she had the leisure. However it contained so much information, an overdose if you could get such a thing. Too many details. Ernie was smart all right. A lot of these gay men were very smart or artistic. Chrissie said that that was ridiculous, they were just like anybody else. Intelligence was determined by the genes. How do you spell the last word, Margaret had asked. But Chrissie had never appreciated her jokes.

'How's your cold?' Ernie was handing her a yellow packet of lozenges. 'Thought you might want to try these. Do miracles for me. Sure enough illness around this year. Psychological. Everyone so defeated by inflation.'

Margaret wondered if Ernie were happy. He looked happy enough. Often he looked, excuse the expression, downright gay. So full of jokes. It took her a while to get used to Ernie, to men like this, to what she had thought was their perversion. But now she knew some of them personally. She found several quite sensitive, thoughtful. They would make perfect husbands. They had more know-how about feelings than a lot of regular men.

'Thanks, Ernie, you're a real honey, you know that.'

'Enough, enough,' he protested. 'One of these days, Margaret, you'll turn my head and we'll have a romance to shock all of San Francisco.'

'How you read my mind,' she grinned back.

Five

Margaret knew she should have kept her mouth shut. Just utter the word 'political' and they wouldn't get back to Scrabble until the tea had frozen over.

'What do you mean "too political"? demanded Chrissie. Her voice rose against Margaret's incessant AM radio, now playing 'Strangers in the Night'. 'How can you be too political when fares on the buses are doubling. Especially if you're so vain that you won't use your senior pass. Those fares'll bankrupt you.'

Margaret raised her palm in protest. Often she wished for a traffic whistle to halt the insults.

'Now don't play Olympic runner with me, Margaret. You know we'd never make it to the wharf without buses. Not until your Irish Sweepstakes tickets come up and we can hire a taxi.'

'But —' Margaret began.

'And they're planning to cut Social Security. Can you believe that? If ever there was a reason I yearned for cold, old Britain, it's the National Health Service.' When Chrissie paused for breath, she noticed her friend's distraction. 'Okay, Okay, so these issues are a little abstract for you. Try violence. mugging, rape.'

'I'm not a stupid woman.' Margaret's tone rose to full strength.

'I know you're not, love. Otherwise we wouldn't be friends.'

'Then let's get back to the game,' Margaret cut her off. The trick of talking with Chrissie was knowing when to check her, letting out the idea, yet heading off the next tirade. 'I think you started this argument because of your Scrabble score.'

'Don't get cheeky with me. I'm ten points ahead.' Chrissie ran her thumb along her broad jaw-bone. 'I'm not a stupid woman either.'

Ignoring her friend, Margaret smiled at her own cleverness,

placing seven tiles across the triple letter and double word scores. 'S-U-B-M-I-T-S.'

'Hmmm,' sniffed Chrissie. 'I don't need to be a psychiatrist to see how that suits your personality.'

'Chrissie MacInnes,' scolded Margaret, 'it's one thing to be a sore loser and quite another to be personally offensive.'

'All right. All right.' Chrissie concentrated, clearly relishing the challenge. 'Now let me see what I have up my sleeve here.'

'Relentless,' thought Margaret, that was the word for Chrissie. Too long for Scrabble, but Chrissie would fit it in somehow. She was always arguing. Relentlessly. Stop nuclear power. Provide day care. End racism. Support senior citizens. If Chrissie were such a socialist why hadn't she stayed in her own country? Where did Chrissie get her energy? And her certainty? Margaret knew she herself was no piece of fluff. However Chrissie seemed to have an opinion — a strong opinion, even — on issues Margaret didn't even know were issues.

Margaret remembered their meeting thirty years before, just after Bill had left her and she got the job at Mummer's. Chrissie had been cool at first, as only the Scots can be. Checking her out, with such scrutiny that Margaret sometimes worried there might be grime beneath her fingernails. Of course Chrissie was looking deeper than that. She was examining Margaret's integrity. When it became apparent that Margaret wasn't going to vote against the union (frankly, Margaret did think most labor leaders were thugs, after her experience with Bill's friends), Chrissie became more friendly. She invited Margaret to Sunday dinner. Margaret said she couldn't leave the kids. So Chrissie invited herself over to their apartment and brought the dinner. After that, Margaret began to wonder if Chrissie's heart had any bounds. She helped find a special school for Rob. She loaned Margaret money for a dozen Christmases and babysat when she went out with a procession of men. She would probably take in Slocum if the handsome minister whisked her away. Margaret often tried to get Chrissie to come on a double date. However her friend had no time for these fellows. Vaguely she referred to someone during the war or before the war, someone dead.

That was one of the few things Chrissie kept to herself. Margaret was just as glad she hadn't opened up that part. She feared she might drown looking all the way into Chrissie.

Chrissie was staring at the Scrabble Board.

'Miss MacInnes,' Margaret sighed in her deepest voice, which she found still, somehow, unpleasantly reedy. 'Are you waiting for your ship to come in? What is the matter with you?'

'Fundraising for Marissa,' Chrissie spoke absently. 'It takes so much time to nickle and dime people. Three days to organize a film showing where we net maybe five, six hundred dollars. Hours and hours of doorbell ringing. In this neighborhood throwing rocks through windows is the only way to get attention.'

Margaret sipped her cold tea and waited. There was no stopping Chrissie, no playing Scrabble, when she was preoccupied. Actually, her own mind wasn't on the game, either. Margaret was worrying about Gudrun, about that nasty bruise under her eye last week. She and Chrissie always had a hard time talking about Gudrun's 'evening companion work'. For herself, Margaret understood that Gudrun needed the money to support her mother. And, as Chrissie said often enough, what was the difference between marriage and high-class whoring? Margaret often wondered if Gudrun wanted to talk about this work. But she waited for Gudrun to bring it up. And when she didn't, Margaret didn't. She felt just as reserved on the topic with Chrissie, out of loyalty or embarrassment or both.

Margaret tried to relax back into the white arm chair. The mock wool upholstery matched the couch and the slightly less comfortable recliner on which Chrissie was perching. Chrissie never seemed to sit, to give the sense she might stay more than ten minutes. This white suite plus the Scandia coffee table and the floor lamp, belonged to the apartment house. Margaret gave away her own furniture when she moved into this studio. It had been so over-sized, so family-sized and out of date. Anyway, this made for a much classier set-up. Plenty of people rented their furniture. She didn't like to think about it that way. Made her feel like she was living in a model home. Still, plenty of people in the city — even rich people like Mr Poulos from the drug store — rented furnished apartments.

The room was decorated with remnants of another life — the bowling ball lamp that Michael had made in metalwork classes. The afghan she had knitted the month after Bill left her. Knicknacks she and Janey had collected from Woolworth's and Newberry's and trips to the shore. San Simeon Castle. A gilded bear from their first visit to Berkeley. And lots of turtles. On the back wall she had hung a print of ballerinas, all orange and brown, dancing in a strange, faint light. Janey had given her the picture one Christmas. On a shelf near the space heater were a set of miniature fireplace tools — the six-inch brush, shovel and poker (scale model perfect) — which the boys had won at a fair. And that mirror was hers, Grandma's mirror they always called it. No one knew if Grandma had ever seen it, however there was something about the thing — a section fuzzy and washed-out — which made you look twenty years older.

The Murphy bed was tucked in the wall behind a discreet natural wood door which looked as if it closed on another room instead of a closet. The window opened to Geary Street, to the blinking lights and incessant noise. Margaret glanced out now to find Roberto walking with his two daughters, the three of them poking each other and laughing. Yes, it did surprise her how many people she knew, how well she knew them. Maybe this wasn't quite the community that Reverend Bentman described, but it *was* a neighborhood.

Slocum growled in her sleep, rolling over on Margaret's feet and drawing her attention back to the Scrabble board. She saw that Chrissie was still distracted, still lost in her fund-raising schemes. She had learned when to surrender.

'So how much have you collected so far?' she asked.

'Twenty thousand dollars,' Chrissie said tersely.

'Whew, that sounds like a fortune to me. You could fund a lot of your social service projects with twenty thousand dollars.'

'Don't be naïve,' said Chrissie. 'Jake Carson has spent forty thousand dollars and still has twice that much left in his coffers.'

'But where does he get that kind of money?' asked Margaret, startled. 'Is he a rich man?'

'Well, first of all, he's getting support from those wealthy folks up on Sutter and Pine. The city has arranged it so the Tenderloin can't vote as a block.' She tried not to sound didactic, but she didn't know how much Margaret understood.

'Everyone has a right to donate,' Margaret said firmly.

'Aye, he's also got the realtors behind him. Development begins with lining Jake Carson's pocket. Legally or illegally.'

'How do you know?' Margaret challenged. She wanted to tell Chrissie that she had met him through Kevin and that Carson seemed an able, energetic man. Then she thought better of mentioning Kevin's name.

'We know,' answered Chrissie, 'because, thank God, everybody has to register campaign contributions.'

'Chrissie, you really hate this man,' declared Margaret 'and you don't even know him.'

Chrissie stared, as if to determine the source of such wild innocence. Finally she spoke; 'I know what he's done. Torn apart streets of low income housing for 'tourist hotels', campaigned on a —'

'But have you ever *met* the *man*?'

'Who needs to? Politicians have an intimate effect on your life whether or not you meet them. And if we had been properly introduced, do you think he'd be walking around with two eyes?'

'Chrissie, don't be ridiculous.'

'You're the one who's ridiculous,' snapped Chrissie, 'sitting here in this cosy nest of memorabilia. How long do you think *this* building will last if he gets his International Trade Fraternity? This very block is targeted.'

Awakened by the noise, Slocum shook herself nervously and ambled to the kitchenette.

'Targeted,' tsked Margaret. 'You make it sound like a war.'

'It *is* a war!' exclaimed Chrissie. 'It's a matter of basic . . .' She stopped, noticing Margaret consider Michael's portrait. Eighteen years old in his new Army uniform, a proud infantryman like his father before him, a dead teenager, like so many after him.

'You think *he* was fighting for this kind of world?' Chrissie asked gently. 'A world in which his seventy-year-old mother gets thrown out on the street by manufacturing giants from Germany and Yugoslavia and Japan. Do you think he wanted this?'

'Could we change the topic?' asked Margaret. 'Maybe another time. But not now.'

Chrissie moved over the arm of the chair and cradled her old friend, hoping to quell the feelings. Feelings, Margaret had so many feelings that they streamed from her like hair from Medusa. Chrissie had fewer feelings because she had learned early. Learned what came of opening your heart, of letting in people who could die there, taking bits of you with them over the years, every time you remembered them.

Margaret rested her aching head against Chrissie's arm, crying softly and breathing in the lavender cologne. Chrissie hunched over Margaret, rocking her and staring out at the lights flashing up from Geary Street. She knew that if she were a better woman, a kinder woman, she would say she was sorry, would do anything to comfort Margaret now. But she was too irritated that Margaret couldn't see past her nose to her own self-interest. Imagine supporting a man like Jake Carson. Imagine — no, there would not be further debate tonight. Margaret seemed like a bird in her ample arms. Such frailty made Chrissie feel resigned about her own physical strength. She tried to mark her breaths to Margaret's, patiently waiting out the sobs.

When Margaret became quiet, Chrissie drew away, saying, 'Just don't expect it to come through on your Irish Sweepstakes tickets.'

'What?' Margaret sat up, patting her hair in place. 'Expect what?'

'Our trip to Hawaii.' Chrissie rubbed the arthritic knuckles on her left hand. 'My Dad did the pools in Edinburgh for forty-five years and all it got him was a deaf ear from my mother's shouting.'

HOT CONTEST IN DISTRICT C
RACE, HOUSING ISSUES FLARE
DOWNTOWNERS SPLIT ON SUP ELECTION

No avoiding it, thought Margaret on Friday morning as she scanned the headlines. People were going mad over this election. Kevin and Douglas had been fighting the entire week. Ernie supported Marissa. So did Roberto. Mr Poulos and Mr Gleason favored Carson. 'A bright, ambitious man,' they each agreed. In fact when they started arguing with Mrs Dougal yesterday morning, Margaret feared she wouldn't get any paying customers for half-an-hour. You couldn't budge them from the counter. And the racket! Slocum joined in with a long howl that might have razed the building.

Margaret was fed up. She agreed with Roger Bentman who said that one's political position was one's own and it wasn't a democratic duty to foist it on every passerby. She was even refreshed to hear from Crazy Captain George. He wasn't voting for anybody, he said in a high voice which was as wispy as the grey hairs escaping beneath his sailor's cap, because if you registered to vote, you got stuck with jury duty. He didn't have time for jury duty. Too busy building his model ships, living his life, to be cooped up in some stuffy court at City Hall.

Chrissie arrived for lunch brewing with excitement. 'Have you seen the latest poll?'

'No.' Margaret frowned, because she didn't want to spend her whole lunch hour on the topic and because she knew that Kevin had just descended from his office and was browsing somewhere among the foreign magazines.

'Well, cold fish, friend of mine, she's winning!'

'Nice.' Margaret slipped on her raincoat. 'I feel like some hot soup today. How about Salamagundi's? Or do you think it will be too crowded?'

'Don't play passive-aggressive with me,' said Chrissie.

'Another of your night school psychology terms?' asked Margaret, hoping that she could keep Chrissie arguing about the value of the community college until they made it out the door.

'She's winning,' Chrissie couldn't hold it back, 'by a good ten per cent. If we can keep up this pace, all the money in Montgomery Street won't do a thing for him.'

'Just a minute,' Margaret called over her shoulder as she walked back to remind Douglas Sinclair that she was leaving.

He sat in the end office like a dour reference librarian, making busy in his correspondence with foreign distributors. Margaret always thought Sinclair had missed his calling. He was business-man enough to set up the shop, but he'd never turn much of a profit. His heart was in the content not the cost of his journals. Yes, Margaret could see him at the Library of Congress. She knocked on the door frame and waved. He nodded goodbye.

'But,' Chrissie persisted from the front desk, 'the TV debate did it. Showed him for the weasel . . .'

Margaret did not hear her friend. She was staring directly at Kevin Sinclair, his face turned away from the magazine rack on the far side of the shop, with the darkest expression she had ever seen on the young man.

Margaret stalked back to Chrissie, her shoulders rigid against the argument to follow.

Six

Four hours of folding letters and licking stamps at Marissa's headquarters — glorified name for an abandoned storefront — and Chrissie still had eight hours work ahead this evening. She should slow down. She should take a more regular schedule at Mummer's. Margaret was right. Still, there was so much to do. And resting made her twitchy. She had intended to go home and lie down for a spell before her night shift at the café, but she found her normally sensible brown brogues walking toward Union Square.

Fresh air would do her good. Here was a different sort of resting. She would bathe in this gifted hour of sunshine until the windy late September darkness drove her arthritic joints inside.

Passing David's Delicatessen, she could smell the Cohen's kitchen from Edinburgh. She had loved playing with Annie and Abe Cohen. Best, she had loved tasting their family's exotic food. Mother, never very keen on 'other people's food', always said you could eat what the Jews cooked. They were clean people. Not sloppy like the Italians. And Father used to tell gruesome stories about Chinese woman chopping off their fingers in the chow mein. Working-class people don't take kindly to immigrants. Chrissie had experienced that herself when she came to America. Although she had long ago discarded her parents' dreadful prejudices, she still couldn't eat chow mein without closing her eyes.

City smells. Chrissie knew there were city smells, like country smells of damp pine needles. City smells of cologne and aftershave the closer you got to the St Francis Hotel. Leather and polish in the fancy shops. Outside, exhaust fumes and rotten produce. City services were slowing down on the outside, noticeable to people who walked the streets or lived on them. Of course it could be worse; she sniffed. Pee in the gutters. And they used to dump garbage along

Bracket Walk. Pee in the streets and, yes, before the exhaust, there was a lot of horseshit.

Bullshit. Look at these window displays. How much did they expect you to swallow? It took Mr Poulos a week to figure out why people laughed at the front window of his drug store. The 'Promise Her Anything' Arpège poster next to the 'New, Improved Pregnancy Testing Kit'. Then these damn fashion windows. Of course she had never been one for fashions. She liked to think of herself as a rough-hewn woman, militantly plain while Margaret was often garish. Well, she did admire the tenacity with which Margaret kept up with the fashions, especially since her friend had managed it all from sales. But she didn't see much use in fashions for her more modest, no, reserved self.

Chrissie looked across Geary Street to Macy's window. Some of these new 'styles' were enough to make you vomit. These weird, punky clothes, nothing short of grotesque. Mannequins with purple hair, carrying whips and belts. Ernie had told her it was a new vogue, this sado-masochism. As if there weren't enough pain in the world.

Afternoons were the hardest for Margaret. She was alert enough in the mornings when the patrons were brisk and cheerful. Afternoons were more sporadic. She couldn't count on anyone particular until four thirty and then there was such a rush she might as well be a coin box on the street. Twenty cents *Examiner;* sixty cents *New York Times;* one dollar *Newsweek.* One dollar. She remembered it when it was thirty five cents not so long ago. Sometimes a whole hour might pass without anything like a conversation. That's why she liked waitressing better. There was always someone to talk to while waiting for the orders. Remarkable how deep they got into each other's lives at Mummer's. Gudrun's hooking; Chrissie's feuding. So much intimacy between the courses. Family sagas; birth control advice; stupid jokes. Also, she had liked Mummer's muzak better. Certainly the popular songs were livelier than Sinclair's droning classical records. She had to thank the café for Chrissie. How else would she have become acquainted with someone so different? But Chrissie, for all her radical notions, was an utterly trustworthy friend. Loyal. The kind of person who watched out for you. Wasn't it Chrissie who found Margaret this job when her legs were giving out?

Work in a news shop: it had seemed so ironic, as if ink were in her veins. Selling papers was what Pop had done. Her earliest memories were of the teens and twenties in New York, minding the shack with Pop. Talk about working with the public! Pop had it down perfectly. And did he ever rake in tips at Christmas. She did, too. Mom didn't like her working outside in the snow, but Margaret loved being with Pop, playing partner, fetching *The Atlantic Monthly, The Journal, The New York Times* (what would Pop have said if he had known it would go to sixty cents?), *Scribners, The Saturday Evening Post.* She learned to be quick and to smile at the customers. 'Tom Conroy's girl,' she overheard a gentleman say, 'that Tom Conroy's girl is smart.'

'Shouldn't you be in school, young lady?' Mr Wardour asked once.

Margaret rolled her big eyes toward her father.

'Here she gets a superior education,' Pop chuckled. 'Look at all the things she reads about — politics and business. Say, honey, run down to the deli and get me some coffee and a Devil Dog. Two Devil Dogs. And a hot chocolate for yourself.'

They had to keep this conspiracy from Mom who wanted her daughters getting the kind of schooling she never had. Neither she nor Tom.

Yet Pop was right about what she learned from the headlines. Teddy Roosevelt. Sarah Bernhardt. Suffragists. Anarchists. The First World War. Look at the people she met — world travelers, captains of industry, philosophers, kings. Well, maybe not kings, but a few deposed princes from unpronounceable countries in central Europe. Tom's shack was more than a place where news was sold. It was a place where news was made. Plans laid. Pipedreams insulated.

'Margaret.' A voice from the present. 'Margaret. Come in-n-n, Margaret.' It was Kevin.

She knew he was only teasing. But he made her nervous. For all his sweetness, he cared about how the store was run. Anyone in his position would care.

'Sorry about that. Just a little day-dreaming,' she admitted. Her attention was drawn by the stiffness with which he held a brown paper bag.

'Getting colder and colder,' he said abruptly, his usually rosy cheeks growing redder. 'Winter comes earlier every year.'

'If you don't sound like an old man . . .' She spoke fondly, regarding him with curiosity.

He was silent, fiddling with the Scotch Tape which secured the brown bag.

'The question is,' she said lightly, 'Are *you* all here today.'

'Just day-dreaming.' He winked and looked more himself. 'Listen Margaret, this is a book. Someone will pick it up later this afternoon.'

She nodded, wondering, still, at his nervousness.

'Well, not to get too sentimental about this, it's for an old school teacher of mine. Very sick. Up at San Francisco General. And her son said he'd drop by to pick it up. Agatha Christie. She was, is, her favorite writer. Shouldn't act like Mrs Hartley's going to die or something. Anyway, he's a short guy with red hair and a beard and he'll ask you for the package. Hartley. Mrs Hartley's son.'

'Kevin, you're a real sweetie, you know that?' Margaret noticed how like Rob he was, with that grin. She reached out and patted the young man's hand, then slipped his book under the counter. 'I'll keep it right here until he comes.'

'Thanks, Margaret,' Kevin said, putting on his heavy, tweed coat. 'And if you see Dad, tell him I've gone for the day.'

He bent over to pat Slocum. The dog, who was in one of her indifferent moods, issued only the slightest whimper of pleasure.

Watching him go, Margaret again wondered why no one appreciated Kevin. Yesterday Roberto had attacked his 'self-interested politics'. Even Ernie called him 'a bit of a *schlemeil*'. The saddest insults came from his own father. Shame they had to fight; Margaret pondered this at least once a day. Douglas Sinclair was a decent man with an ironic goodwill toward everyone except his son.

What was it about families that created such rifts? Here she was, closer to each man than they could ever be to each other. Thank God her own family were different, still, they weren't perfect. Why did the kids choose to live so far away? She tormented herself with that question. Why were both children in such frozen, northern places? She wondered whether she had driven them away, whether her intensity had made them settle so near the North Pole. Michael had always been different. Sweet, sunny Michael. He never seemed to brood as much as the others. You could see it in the family pictures: Rob and Janey always had frowns on their faces, but Michael's eyes shone easily. Everything was so simple for him, even that terrible decision of entering the army. He could get training there, could finance a technical education, could defend his country, fight as his father had fought. It was Michael, only Michael, who continued to see Bill after the divorce. If Bill was the one who applauded Michael for enlisting, Janey was the one who challenged him. The fights they had that year! Janey exhausted from anti-war marching, moving alone to Canada. (When she said you didn't need a man to resist the war and the draft, Margaret wondered if the girl were a little crazy as well as headstrong.) Michael insisting on defending democracy. Enough to bring down the roof. It did tear the family apart as Janey went off to British Columbia that spring and Michael left for Saigon at the end of the summer.

The glass door opened. In walked Roger Bentman, smiling. He was such an attractive man, probably in his mid-sixties: silver hair; a full, usually florid face; broad shoulders; husky voice. Once, Margaret had wondered wistfully why they hadn't met thirty years before. Almost immediately, she realized that a young minister wouldn't have had much to do with an ignorant waitress who had dropped out of high school. True, since his wife died, he had been friendly. But she knew she was just the clerk behind the cash register. He had to buy his newspapers somewhere.

'And how is my lady of the headlines this afternoon?' He was smiling even more broadly now.

Embarrassed Margaret dropped her eyes. Finally, she answered, 'Better off than the headlines, I suspect.'

'Yes, yes. Terrible this violence around the election.'

'Did you read yesterday that five windows displaying Marissa Washington signs had been broken?'

'Yes, yes,' he sighed. 'Ugly, racist business.'

'Yeah, racist,' came a voice from the back of the store. Douglas Sinclair emerged, buttoning a brown cardigan around his small paunch. 'They hate her because she's black all right. But also because she wants to keep downtown a place where people can afford to pay rent.' Sinclair seemed to enjoy slipping unsuspected into conversations like an omnipresent conscience.

'Well, you can hardly call the Tenderloin a sanctuary,' said Bentman.

'I sure can,' shot back Sinclair. 'Look at all the pensioners who live around here. Maybe not under the best conditions. So improve the conditions; don't take away their homes.'

'Certainly there are better places, like suburban subsidized housing,' Bentman tried again.

'Off in Nowhere Land,' said Sinclair. 'And it won't just be the pensioners who are kicked out. The shop couldn't survive a boom in rent.'

Margaret stared in surprise.

'This place is an institution,' Bentman declared. 'Why, the mayor would make it into a landmark before she let it be torn down.'

'We get a few more developers like Carson in there,' Sinclair said, 'and landmarks won't be worth two cents.'

'Well, I can guess what's in your hand,' said Bentman.

He nodded and held out a sign: 'Marissa Washington, The People's Supervisor'. Marissa's handsome face shone out at them.

Margaret thought the photograph was a good one, managing to convey her fifty years as an accumulation of friendly wisdom. Her wide brown eyes, set off by the high cheekbones, lent a delicacy to her tough, confident expression.

'Thought I'd set it in the far window,' he said to Margaret. 'So if they start throwing rocks, you won't get hit.'

'I appreciate your consideration,' she said dryly. When Reverend Bentman left, she would have a talk with him. What did he think Kevin would do when he saw the sign?

'You're really concerned, aren't you?' Bentman regarded Sinclair seriously. He had always been put off — intimidated — by the gruffness of the shopkeeper. Now he looked sympathetic.

37

The door opened between them, admitting a small, bearded man. Margaret noticed his red hair and she smiled in greeting.

'You must be Mrs Hartley's son,' she said.

He seemed to look through her.

'You're here to pick up the package from Mr Sinclair.' she said helpfully, knowing the lad must be feeling distressed about his mother.

'Yes, thank you,' he said quietly.

She handed him the brown bag. 'I hope she recovers soon.' Her voice was loud enough for everyone to register Kevin's generosity.

'Thanks.' He nodded shyly and left the store.

'I hadn't heard about this threat on Marissa Washington's life,' Roger Bentman was saying to Sinclair.

Margaret had read about it in the first edition of the *Examiner* that afternoon. Marissa had received an anonymous letter saying that she should lay off the developers, or she wouldn't 'have a voice left to sing with'. What crude language, thought Margaret, like something out of a George Raft movie. Jake Carson himself decried such intimidation in the same article.

Margaret was getting worried for Chrissie. Spending every spare minute at these organizing doo-dah's, she could get hit by a bomb or a bullet. Margaret was having second thoughts about attending that rally at Glide Memorial Church tomorrow evening. How had Chrissie talked her into spending Saturday night at a meeting?

'Maybe you could do something, Reverend?' suggested Sinclair.

'One can't take political stands in church.'

'No, of course not,' Sinclair was curt. 'However you can take stands against brutality.'

'Surely.' Bentman strained for patience. 'I understand the issue is of real urgency to the downtown community.'

Margaret thought she saw Sinclair wince. He recovered quickly. 'Whatever you can do, Reverend, whatever.'

Margaret tried to keep step with Chrissie down Taylor Street, grateful that her friend was in a pensive mood rather than a lecturing one. She had almost told Chrissie she was too tired to go out this Saturday night, however she knew that would endanger their friendship. She also knew she was stalling out of laziness or fear or both. So she had locked a cranky Slocum in the apartment — all right to nose around the street in the afternoon, Margaret told the dog, but anything could happen at night — then she met Chrissie in the lobby of their apartment house for this brisk march down to Glide Memorial Church.

As they walked, Chrissie considered how good this meeting would be for Margaret. It would give her a chance to find out other people shared her problems. Margaret had the right instincts. She was just a little slow on political connection. Chrissie glanced over as her friend greeted Little Pete and she noticed how the streetlights made Margaret's eyeshadow slightly irridescent. Why she insisted on caking that godawful mess on her aging face, Chrissie would never understand. That and the mascara which ran in the rain or in the tears which came with miraculous naturalness to Margaret. She was a fine-looking woman without all the goop. You'd think she were auditioning for Madame Butterfly.

'This doesn't feel like a church,' Margaret whispered as they entered.

'Aye, more like a cross between a New Age conference and a sales convention.' Chrissie made no effort to lower her voice.

Margaret stared wordlessly at a line of tables covered with pamphlets about rent control and whales and lesbians and holistic healing.

'Well, if it isn't Margaret! So you do leave that shop once a year.'

Margaret turned around, startled, to find Ernie sitting under a sign with circles and arrows and the words 'Gay Freedom'.

'Nice to see you, Ernie.' Margaret composed herself by recalling something familiar. 'Those lozenges were sent from heaven.'

He grinned, 'No, just from your little fairy.'

Margaret blushed and to hide her embarrassment, she studied the table. Then she felt Chrissie tugging at her coat.

'Come on. Come on,' urged Chrissie. 'We'll never get seats. We can read propaganda at the break. Hi, Ernie.' She raised her hand in impatient salute. 'Bye, Ernie.'

Margaret followed her friend into the sanctuary, marvelling at how professional Chrissie was at all of this. She had been right about the crowds. The pews were packed. So many black faces, Margaret was surprised and then taken aback by her surprise. As they searched for seats, Margaret felt at once daring to be at a political rally and guilty to have made them late.

Chrissie surveyed the crowd with satisfaction. She saw old Mrs Dougal twitching for the meeting to start and sweet Arthur Chow studying the program. It was at public moments like this that she knew her deepest passion and sense of possibility. Right now she felt hope not only for Marissa and the neighborhood, but for a certain part of herself that was usually closed.

'Do you know that person?' Margaret pointed to a tall black man waving broadly to Chrissie from a front pew.

Chrissie peered and broke into a grin. 'Gus!' She waved back. 'Marissa's husband. Looks like he's got a couple of seats for us. Ringside.'

As they made their way down the aisle. Margaret was astonished by how many people Chrissie knew. She might be Marissa Washington herself.

'Hello there, Margaret.' A familiar voice. Of course, Roberto. Three rows ahead was Douglas Sinclair, seated next to Harold Lawson and autographing the cast on his arm.

Applause. Whistles. Dimming lights. Chrissie took Margaret's elbow and hurried her to their pew. They sat just as Marissa walked out on stage.

She was a big, beautiful woman, observed Margaret. Big, not in a fat way or even a stocky, muscular way, but grand. She wore her hair in a full Afro, the elegant curls accentuated by large gold hoop earrings. She smiled at the applause. Then she stood tall, clapping in response. Finally she held up one pale palm to hush the crowd.

'Broken windows,' she began in a bass voice. 'One broken arm. Many broken promises. And I ask you, what is next? We know from the strength of these assaults that we, ourselves, are strong.'

Whistles, applause. Again a raised palm to quell the crowd.

'Together — poor people, old people, blacks, whites, gays — together our oppressions become power because they know the depth of our protest.'

Margaret looked around at the rapt faces and wondered if it had been this stirring with Martin Luther King. No, she was probably getting carried away.

'So I know that the threats on my life are the threats on our movement.'

Boos; hisses; roars of anger.

'Threats against the momentum of what we are trying to accomplish. Make this city habitable again. Preserve it for people's lives rather than for corporate profits.'

Catcalls. Clapping. Footstomping. A standing ovation.

Margaret glanced back to Douglas Sinclair's attentive face. She could see traces of Kevin. They had virtually the same face if you were to pull back the wrinkles, lift the chin and color out the grey. She recalled Kevin's eagerness as he had introduced Jake Carson to her last week. She worried.

Sensing her stare, Douglas Sinclair smiled. Shyly, she smiled too, and turned back to Marissa Washington.

Seven

Saturday afternoon was usually reserved for pinochle. Today, however, Margaret insisted on attending the Pray for Peace Vigil at Brotherhood Church: Roger Bentman's answer to the troubles facing their downtown community. Chrissie, who believed in letting people make their own mistakes, simply declined the invitation. Tolerating Bentman's sweet civility in the news shop was one thing, but voluntarily submitting to it for an entire afternoon was quite beyond her.

Instead, Chrissie tried to balance her check book. Maybe it would surprise her this month. Within half-an-hour, she found herself staring at the increasingly close walls of her small apartment. If Margaret's studio was old-womanish and cluttered, Chrissie's was spare and sensible — like her image to the outside world. Plain green rug, dark blue furniture, clean surfaces. The only visible intimacies were a silver brush and comb and a small picture of her brother James in a tin frame. The white walls were bare. She had removed the apartment house pictures and, unlike Margaret, had never found replacements. Simple, orderly. Chrissie liked her home.

But the damn rain intruded today. Quiet. Incessantly quiet. Drops whispered against her windows. Streams of water patterned the panes in maddening jigsaws. Rain always floated her back to Edinburgh. This kind of soft steadiness was enough to suffocate her, to draw in those old feelings of frustration and loneliness: the guilt at wanting to leave; the impatience until enough money was saved for the ship. She had hoped that in the ship, immersed for days, she would be cleansed of that water torture. Drip, drip, drip. At least in the ocean you could see it all at once. You could swim in it. Sail through it. To safety. Yet, even forty years later and half-the-world away, she still felt imprisoned inside the drip, drip, dripping. She needed to go out in the rain, to get wet, to prove to herself she would not drown.

42

Just too depressing to sit here alone on a chilly Saturday balancing an almost overdrawn account. Chrissie stood up, brushed off her skirt and walked over to the coat closet. If she stayed here one more minute, she would head straight for the brandy. Easy enough to become an alcoholic. Sometimes she could see her father's face on every drunk in the street. Bracket Walk was not so different from certain parts of the Tenderloin. You had to keep busy, she reminded herself as she double-locked her apartment door. You had to stay useful.

Chrissie set off toward headquarters. Although this wasn't her shift, there was bound to be some envelope-stuffing. As she walked along Eddy, she considered what a hodge-podge this neighborhood was — liquor stores, bars, TV repair shops, laundries. She paused at one doorway, 'The Redeemer Mission', out of business in an official capacity, but someone had used the doorway as a refuge recently, judging from the sherry bottle and cigarette butts.

She found herself crossing the street. She knew the 'good' and 'bad' sides of the street. On Leavenworth, for example, the east side was safer to walk on then the west, but only between Turk and Eddy. Between Turk and Golden Gate, it was just the opposite, so she had learned to zig zag around the Tenderloin.

Thus absorbed, Chrissie didn't see Captain George until he yelled hello from a doorstep. She waved swiftly, setting her mind back to Marissa's accounts. It was easier to try balancing Marissa's books, less depressing, possible to share the outrage when pockets were overdrawn. She enjoyed the spirit in Marissa's office, busy with all sorts of people — that paraplegic woman Karen, Roberto, Marissa's old friends from the Black Caucus. Gus Washington often dropped over from his law office six blocks away. Of course there was Marissa's presiding good humor.

This dark afternoon, Chrissie let herself into the office with her own key. She felt honored to be one of the four people given keys. Security had been tight since the bomb threats. Chrissie switched on the light and felt frost gather along her collarbone. They had been warned never to enter the office alone. One person in the storefront was too vulnerable. The fluorescent noise seemed to bounce off the old classroom chairs and makeshift desks. No cameraderie this afternoon, Chrissie thought, wishing that she had been smart enough to wear a sweater under her coat. Damn arthritis. She pulled out the space heater. That would take off the chill. And soon she was tapping away on the calculator Douglas had donated.

Chrissie glanced at a pile of papers on the next desk. Clippings from the past two weeks of the campaign. Both candidates had received extensive coverage because of the broken windows and rumors of larger violence. In yesterday's *Examiner,* under an anxious headline, Marissa's face shone like an equanimous Buddha. Well, perhaps there was a line of worry around the mouth.

Chrissie was proud of her friendship with Marissa, whom she had known almost as long as she had known Margaret, yet in such a different way. They had met on the picket line, walking in sympathy with the Southern sit-ins. They had shared an egg salad sandwich, a dill pickle and a warm Coke. Right away, she knew Marissa was a smart woman. Both she and her husband Gus were going to Hastings Law School at night. Unlike a lot of ambitious couples, they didn't plan to leave the city. They wanted to stick around and change it. That's why Marissa was giving up her teaching. She could do more as a lawyer and maybe someday as a politician. How had Chrissie got involved in civil rights, Marissa wanted to know. How, indeed, Chrissie, herself, had wondered, re-membering her parents' exhortations about Italian and Chinese food. However Rajid had been an important part of her life. Someday she might tell Marissa and Margaret about Rajid. Someday she might allow herself to think more about Rajid.

Studying the newspaper picture now, Chrissie marvelled that Marissa seemed not to have aged since those marches twenty-five years before. Her face had grown stronger. And her hair had sprung into a wide Afro which softened her dramatic bone structure and deepened those intense brown eyes. The notion that anyone would want to harm Marissa filled Chrissie with dread. It was as crazy as wanting to hurt Margaret.

The rain pelted heavily on the wide front window. Hail?

44

Ping! In back of her, Chrissie heard a sudden ping! Ping! Startled, she turned to find rain dripping from the ceiling into an aluminium pan. Dampness. Dampness closed around her joints. She thought of wet Edinburgh autumns. She remembered moments from that terrible last day with Rajid: boys clomping down the cobbled streets; the taunts; the rocks; the Royal Infirmary.

'Enough.' Chrissie spoke away the ghosts. Now she was too conscious of working alone, too wary. She would return tomorrow, which was much more sensible because Gus had the rest of the accounts. She distracted herself from danger as she filed the checks; turned off the calculator; stored the space heater and locked the door behind her.

4:30 pm. Maybe she would catch Harvey at the Clift Hotel before he started playing at 5:30. Maybe they could have a beer together. Harvey was always good company.

4:45 pm, an in-between city time. Shoppers heading home. Tourists walked briskly through the light rain back to their hotels. A few industrious hookers already stood in the shadows. Chrissie waved to Roberto, who smiled at her between customers. 'On' when everybody else was 'off', Roberto thrived on the coming and going, cracks in the city's day. As Chrissie passed Sinclair's shop, she peeped in the window to find Douglas contentedly smoking his pipe and bent over a copy of the same green paperback he was reading yesterday. What was it? Oh, yes, Virgil's *Aeneid.* Bright man. A little intellectual, though.

Bernie, the doorman, was on duty outside the Clift. Like a ringmaster in his fancy hat and long brown coat, he paced the taxis and suitcases and befuddled hotel guests. He always had time for a little sarcastic flirting with Chrissie.

'How's the old battleaxe this afternoon?' he asked.

'Strong enough to go a round with you,' she laughed. 'And don't you forget it.' She considered how he would never treat Margaret like this. Not Lady Margaret. No one was indelicate in front of her. Not that she was all that delicate. Still, she was a lady all right. Sometimes it bothered Chrissie how much niçer people were to Margaret. Didn't they know she had feelings too? Oh, what the hell was getting into her tonight? The sooner she had a drink with Harvey, the better off she and the rest of the world would be.

Bernie reached into the pocket where he deposited his taxi bribes. 'This is for Marissa,' he said, handing her a ten. 'I heard about those busted windows.'

'Thanks.' Chrissie smiled. 'Want a receipt? Tax deductible, you know.'

'Nope,' he said. 'It's from an unofficial account.'

'Right then,' she patted his padded shoulder and proceeded through the lobby, waving to Agnes at Reception, but not stopping to chat.

The lobby was set as a tearoom in the afternoons. The civilized clinking of china was almost over now. Chrissie recalled drinking tea in the Caledonian with James and his fiancée to celebrate their engagement, the first and only time she had ever entered the posh Caledonian Hotel. To think that she came to the Clift every two or three weeks now. Not their usual clientèle, perhaps, but she paid for her drinks with ready cash.

Upstairs in the Redwood Room, a new waiter puttered around preparing the *hors d'oeuvres* table. Otherwise she would have reached in and helped herself to the meatballs. If Harvey were here, she'd get enough for dinner. No sooner had she thought about him than he wandered over, smoothing back his black hair. He moved irridescently in a green satin smoking jacket.

'Two Heinekens,' he called to the waitress. The young woman nodded carefully, as if her false eyelashes might detach with too much activity.

Chrissie made herself comfortable against the wall. She stared up at her favorite Klimt reproduction in a giant redwood frame. She loved drinking in this room, pretending she were lounging in a museum. (Margaret always teased her, 'How can you like the M&M Bar *and* the Redwood Room? Don't you find the Redwood Room a little classy for your "politics"?') Truth was, Chrissie could ignore the bourgeois patrons because the nostalgia was so heavy. The soft lights. Harvey's melancholy songs. This all conjured the happiest days of her life. No, she wasn't going to get soppy. In those times she believed that anything might get done. Now she believed that almost anything might get done. Not such a great change.

'So how is my highland lass?' Harvey made a dreadful attempt at the brogue.

'Tired,' she said, deciding not to remind him again that Edinburgh is a long road from the highlands.

'Would a meatball wake you up?' he asked.

'I wouldn't be ungrateful.' She rested back against the wall and gazed at the elegant ceiling. Yes, almost anything might get done.

Harvey returned just in time for the beers, whisking the check from Chrissie's hand.

'No,' she insisted, 'we're both working people.'

'You treat me to coffee at Mummer's,' he said.

'Coffee is fifty cents,' she declared. 'Beer is two dollars.'

'Down to the penny,' he teased. 'You really are a Scot.' Signing the cheque with an exaggerated flourish, he concluded, 'I bet you didn't get a fifty dollar tip from a Bostonian banker last night to play "The Naughty Lady of Shady Lane".'

'Aye, you can wager I didn't.' Chrissie sucked in the foam. Across the room she noticed Gudrun laughing with the Brisbane chap who had been hanging about Mummer's this week. Chrissie looked back to Harvey, perplexed by her own embarrassment at seeing Gudrun on her other job.

'A toast,' Harvey said in his best cheering-up voice, 'to Marissa's election.'

'To Marissa's survival.' Her tone was bleak.

'Listen, old pal.' He grew serious. 'Uncle Harvey only has fifteen more minutes before he's called to torture the ivories. Tell me what's wrong with you, Ms MacInnes. Where did you run into this wet blanket?'

'Well, I'm worried about the violence.'

'You've lived with that long enough,' he said. 'Marissa too. You're both tough broads.'

'That doesn't mean we want to die with it,' she said, reviewing the bomb threats, Harold Lawson's 'mugging', and the broken windows as if speaking about the danger might purge her fear. Then they tried to talk of other things.

Beep. Beep. Harvey's digital watch. He raised his glass to toast her.

'Here's to the Dark Celt,' he said.

'Here's to the art of music,' she said.

'Right you are.' Her friend smoothed back his hair and made his way to the piano.

Harvey's first number was 'Ye Tak The High Road'. She tried to listen and to appreciate his kindness. However when she looked at the Klimt, she found the gold squares were blurred by tears. Better move along before she made a ripe fool of herself, she thought, wiping her eyes with the tiny cocktail napkin. She pulled out a dollar for the tip. Too depressed to eat the last meatball, she considered how a walk would do her good.

Chrissie ducked out the door, hoping Harvey wouldn't notice. The smoky aroma of Earl Grey tea prevailed as she hurried through the lobby. Bernie was helping some Japanese tourists into a cab, so she just waved goodbye.

Chrissie caught a reflection of herself in a store window. She observed her white hair shining against her dark coat, her sturdy shoulders framing a straight back. Yes, a walk would do her good. How had she slipped into this depression, anyway? As Harvey said, she'd lived here for decades. She knew what to expect. She wasn't some dozy sightseer, swinging a huge purse in front of the pickpockets. Chrissie had walked two blocks down Geary Street before she realized it was still raining. She wiped the tears and rain from her cheeks, pleased to feel the warmth of her face, and shot her black umbrella straight into the cold night air.

Eight

'I'm sure Bentman's sweet on you, Margaret,' said Douglas Sinclair.

'Oh, hush.' She straightened the stack of papers to discharge her nervous energy. 'And what would you know about it?'

'It's as plain as the smile on his ugly face — that big grin he wears whenever he talks to you.'

Reddening, Margaret glanced over her shoulder to make sure no one else was privy to this excruciating conversation.

'He's just a friendly man,' she said. 'He cares a lot about people in the community.'

'He sure doesn't smile at *me* that way,' teased Sinclair. 'And you've been spending plenty of time in the holy house.'

'What do you mean?' She was aware of the red rising up the side of her neck. 'I go once a week, Sunday mornings, a fairly normal American observance.'

'Hmmm, I'd say you were observing more than the service. Listen, honey, I don't want to rile you. I think it's great. Lucky man. Luckier than me. Your pretty head hasn't turned this way in the twenty years you've sat behind that cash register.'

Now Margaret was paralyzed. Was he joking? Once or twice he had said something, more like *implied* something. Never had she taken him seriously. No, no, he was just teasing again. She hoped so. He was a nice enough man, but so dour, so cynical. It sometimes took an entire week to get a laugh out of him. What could he see in her? And what could Roger Bentman see? Certainly no one close to his position or refinement. Of course this was all Douglas Sinclair's way of fooling — of being friendly on the edge of irritation — just his peculiar manner.

'Changing the topic,' she said shakily, 'I've been meaning to mention that sign.'

'We've done pretty well with it so far, eh? Not a crack in

the window.'

'We've had several, um huh, complaints.'

'Offended customers?' Sinclair asked. 'Who? Who had the nerve to tell me what to put in my window?'

'It's not that. But Mr . . .' She paused, wary of his temper.

'Don't waffle,' he demanded, leaning on the counter. He always leaned on something when he was agitated.

Margaret studied the veins splintering violet into his ashen skin. For all his cantankerousness, he had been a real friend to her, helped her through Michael's death and that terrible spell with her gall bladder. Holding in this irritation was no good for anyone. She almost smiled, imagining Douglas Sinclair in one of those yoga relaxation classes, his legs tied in front of him like a pretzel.

'Reverend Bentman had a solution,' she said. 'He thought you might put both signs in the window.'

'We're a news shop,' he snapped, 'not a damn equal access television station.'

'He was only trying to . . .'

'Promote community interest,' Sinclair finished with disgust.

'I was also thinking of Kevin,' Margaret persisted. 'Even though I don't like to get involved in family matters.'

'Kevin is a grown man,' Sinclair said bitterly. 'He's got a right to his lousy judgment. However I'm not going to advertise it in my window.' He was pacing back and forth between the film magazines and the metro newspapers.

'I didn't mean to upset you,' said Margaret.

'You don't mean to upset anyone, woman, that's your trouble. This is an upsetting world. An upsetting neighborhood. You act like you're selling newspapers in fairyland, where everything is honeycomb and hope.' He stopped, noticing the anxiety on her face and the hoarseness in his own voice. 'Listen, Margaret.' He reached over for her hand. 'I didn't mean to upset you.'

'Oh, don't worry, Mr Sinclair.'

'Damn it, will you ever stop calling me "Mr Sinclair"? I'm going out for a drink. Oh, don't give me that concerned face. I know it's only eleven o'clock. The doc said an occasional beer is good for my blood. This one will be good for my

50

temper. I'll be back to relieve you by eleven thirty.'

As Sinclair left, Margaret was covered in mortification. What had got into her? She never stepped into people's personal lives unless she were invited. And she knew Douglas Sinclair had a terrible anger. Hadn't she watched him use it often enough on his son? Why did she speak out of turn? She hated it when he made fun of her. Hated to be considered an innocent old lady. What was wrong with a little optimism anyway? God knows, she hadn't been born into fairyland. If anyone were deluded it was he. Stocking all the bizarre French film magazines that no one bought. While she admired his thoroughness, it annoyed her every time she passed those dusty, aging journals with the morose new wave covers.

Margaret reached down and scratched Slocum behind the ears, hungry for simple affection. The dog sighed deeply and rolled against the woman's feet. Margaret smiled appreciatively at her sleek, well-brushed coat.

What made a person optimistic or cynical, she wondered. Ernie would say it had to do with the stars — with your moon being in Mars or Taurus while you married a Virgo or some such nonsense. Margaret rather thought that temperament had to do with choice, a choice you made about life very early on as a child.

She could pin down her choice to the night she awoke from a loud bang. She was fourteen, alone in the apartment with her sister, and she felt a sudden horrible certainty that she had grown up. Cold premonition made her rise and enter the kitchen where she made a pot of tea. Two hours later, just after 3 am, the police arrived, saying that her parents had died in a mass of tangled iron. They described the streetcar accident down near the vaudeville theatre, however she could not absorb the details. While they talked, she kept crying because she hadn't had a chance to say goodbye. Instead of loss, she felt impatience, as if she were in an empty waiting room where she would remain forever, unable to say goodbye.

She made her choice to continue, to 'survive', as they said nowadays. Sometimes when she thought back on that time, she could hardly bear the grief. Dreadful experience for a fourteen-year-old girl — to be orphaned, to lose everything, to leave school which she was just beginning to love, where Mrs Johnson was counting on her being a great playwright like Lady Gregory. Yet there was never a bad that couldn't be a worse, as Mom would say. It was harder for Sylvia who was only ten. A child can't comprehend disaster. In translating for Sylvia, Margaret herself began to understand. Besides, it was 1923, a time of prosperity in New York. Imagine if it had been a few years later. How would a teenager get a job in a town where family men combed streets for salt and bread? So Margaret was lucky to find her job at the New York City Coffee Shop on Fifth Avenue, just a couple of blocks from the high tone Cornucopia Restaurant where she would work when she was older. She had liked serving the public since the days with Pop in the news shack. For a while, she tried to keep up the writing, scribbling late at night after the apartment was cleaned and Sylvia was tucked in. Eventually, she surrendered to fatigue. Once in a while she thought about Lady Gregory. She supposed that if she had been meant to write, she would have found a way.

A cold whoosh of damp air drew Margaret back to the present. She pulled the afghan around her knees and pressed her feet back into Slocum's fur for warmth. How could she even pretend to be nostalgic about New York? Never had she felt such cold in San Francisco. No, New York was not the city for an older middle-aged person like herself.

Suddenly here was Roberto, handing her a cup of coffee which she hadn't even ordered.

'I saw at the rally that Chrissie's turned you into a radical after all,' he said.

So like Roberto — to insult you with one hand and give with the other. Margaret looked into his dark eyes and saw what she usually saw — glints of green that she imagined as tropical jungles and sparks of yellow, keen as desert sun. Roberto was full of the vitality Margaret associated with his country. She never answered one of Roberto's remarks quickly. She would wait to make contact with those eyes, to find out what she already knew — he was the biggest tease North of the Border.

'That's called "guilt by association",' she volleyed. 'How

do you know I wasn't representing the CIA or Jake Carson's private spy squad?'

'Because neither Carson nor la CIA would be smart enough to hire you.'

'Hi, Gang.' Ernie. Another brush of cold. Ernie looked remarkably chipper for this early in the day. 'Say Margaret, my love, it was good to see you at Marissa's do.'

'Just observing,' she answered.

'For the UN?' he smiled.

'La CIA,' said Roberto. The two men laughed.

Margaret sat back against the wooden slats of her stool which served as an extra spine, and considered how Roberto used to loathe Ernie. A real queer, he had said. Fag germs, keep away from me. Such hostility, she remembered, enough to crack the air. Roberto's macho offended by Ernie's camp. Last year you never would have found them hanging around the shop together. Not for more than five seconds. Now there was some kind of truce. Margaret had never asked why — was it the movement of time or some heroic act? — however the two men were passing friends and political allies. This, she would tell Douglas Sinclair, was what Reverend Bentman meant by 'the downtown community'.

'Did you hear about the attempt on Marissa's headquarters last night?' Roberto's voice had turned urgent. 'It was after midnight and . . .'

Margaret realized she had been telling the truth about observing. She had always been an observer. Ever since the news shack. Maybe she would have been a writer if things had turned out differently. And maybe this was one reason Janey became a poet. That girl was a watcher too. Used to sit patiently while her brothers acted rowdy. Then she would call them together, serve grape juice and tell them stories. Amazing the way the child could make those two hooligans into listeners. Lady Gregory must have been quite an observer herself.

Slocum barked. Roberto and Ernie fell silent as a stranger angled in the door.

Mrs Hartley's son. Margaret smiled, trying to allay the young man's awkwardness. She reached down and eased panting Slocum's back into her usual sprawl.

53

'That's a good girl, right there on my frozen toes.' Slocum settled uneasily in the spot where she had rested for ten years.

Ernie and Roberto resumed their conversation.

'Good morning,' she said. 'How is your mother doing these days?'

'Fine, fine.' He sounded a little less shy, yet still nervous. Except for the red hair, he looked a bit like Michael. The same age, the same short, stocky build. His tattoo was what made her think about it. Two bluish-green snakes wove themselves together from his hand, up his wrist and then under the heavy plaid jacket. So many boys got tattoos as soon as they joined the service. Margaret had warned Michael that he would never get rid of the tattoo as long as he lived. She spoke as if he had long to live in those days when she made more assumptions.

'Is there another b-b-book for my mother?'

Margaret paid close attention, as if her concentration might relax his stammer.

'Of course, of course.' Margaret felt under the counter for the second book which Kevin had left. Slocum wiggled. Margaret drew her hand the length of the animal's golden back.

'Here you go.' She gave him a sealed brown bag. 'And take her my good . . .' He was out the door before she could finish.

Ernie shrugged his shoulders.

'Kevin's high school teacher,' Margaret explained, pleased to say a good word in front of Roberto who hated Kevin. Dear Ernie, with his positive nature, had always accepted the lad. 'She's sick and Kevin has been sending her books.'

'What does he get out of the deal?' frowned Roberto.

'You just don't know the boy.' Margaret was irritated as ever with his implacable judgments.

'Well, I'd sure like to know what's under that plain brown wrapper,' laughed Ernie. 'Must be some kinky old lady.'

'You know,' Margaret said slowly, picking up her feather duster, 'both of you can be very unpleasant.'

The two men laughed as Margaret attended to the imaginary dust on the chewing gum rack and the cigarette case.

'Careful you don't wear off the plastic from the counter,' warned Ernie.

'Or the pretty green feathers off the mop,' offered Roberto.

54

'Haven't you got better things to do?' She didn't want to be abrupt, but she was exasperated that no one even *tried* to appreciate Kevin. 'Or have you both decided on early retirements?'

'Yes, sir, Mama.' Roberto feigned fear and rushed out the door.

'Well, I know where I'm loved.' Ernie followed with an exaggerated flounce.

Margaret repented her temper all the way down to Brotherhood Unitarian Church. Slocum kept a steady, companionable pace. Reverend Bentman's bag lunch lectures were getting popular. Always thirty or forty people. 'Civilized religion,' Gudrun mocked. Margaret liked the variety of poetry or drama or a chapter from a great novel, followed by a discussion about how Art sustained Daily Life. 'Watered-down religion,' Douglas Sinclair scoffed. But then, Sinclair was such an outlandish atheist that he barely permitted *The Christian Science Monitor* into his shop.

The walk to church would clear her head. Why had she been so jumpy lately? Maybe Chrissie was right. Maybe she needed that Hawaiian vacation. She did work eight hours a day, five days a week, fifty weeks a year. Chrissie claimed that was too long for someone her age. Margaret grievously regretted revealing her birthdate to Chrissie. Her friend said that you had to take care of yourself because 'god knows' (using the term 'god' loosely), 'no one else is going to take care of you.' Margaret wondered if there was just a little smugness in Chrissie's independence. She had not gone to the bother of reproducing, only to find her children would not support her anyway. Chrissie never did understand that Margaret didn't think they owed her a thing. Although she missed them, she was proud of their accomplishments. Often she marvelled that this rugged man and this literary woman were her children. What part did she play in their characters which were so different from each other and from her own? Margaret passed a new Vietnamese grocery where packages of odd-looking noodles were displayed in the entryway. Last week this place had been, what, oh, yes, one of those vacant storefronts, the window cracked and seamed with silver electrical tape. Such vigor this neighborhood had. Green plants grew up through the concrete. Family groceries replaced empty hovels. She sighed, relieved that the air was, indeed, clearing her head.

The church was only four blocks away, but the walk could take fifteen minutes, depending on how far the damp had seeped into her bones, depending on how choosey Slocum was about doing her duty. Margaret still felt peculiar bringing the dog to church. But dear Reverend Bentman, who understood that Margaret worried when Slocum roamed the neighborhood, even though she always stayed within a couple of blocks where everyone knew her, suggested that she bring the dog and leave her in the vestibule.

This morning Margaret broke her walk in two places. First at the dry cleaners to pick up her raincoat. She waved to Fayella, who was washing the windows. Margaret respected the pride the Watsons took in their shop. Then she stopped at Petrucci's grocery to buy a chocolate bar for Chrissie and herself tonight. She planned to return home on another route of different errands for she had learned to save energy the way Chrissie saved money. Reverend Bentman wouldn't mind her appearing laden with parcels. He always said Church was meant to be a center of life in the downtown community. He was so tolerant and generous. How Douglas Sinclair had interpreted his small attentions as a *crush* she didn't know.

Brotherhood Unitarian Church stood stalwart in neo-colonial white, an odd reference to stern New England in operatic San Francisco. Inside, Roger Bentman had transformed the austerity with embroidered wall-hangings and photographs of local people. It didn't have the 'political' atmosphere of Glide Memorial Church, Margaret noted with approval; it had more of a homey quality.

She could hear the applause as she reached the sanctuary door. She hurried to her seat in the back row.

'*The Crucible* by Arthur Miller, a study in piety and hypocrisy,' Bentman began. He was so alive at moments like this, as if light radiated from behind his eyes. He embraced everyone in his intelligent, compassionate gaze. He gave a brief smile to Margaret. Was it to her? Embarrassed, she sat stiffly still. She returned to his grey eyes and accepted the attention, nodding modestly. He spoke of witches and communists and all those different ideas that he tied together so well. His ample hands followed the words with gentle affirmation.

'Miller is writing about judgment by association. Think how often we do this in our own lives − in private affairs and public encounters. Let's ask about contemporary social scapegoating. Surely this didn't stop with seventeenth-century witch trials or with the McCarthy hearings in the 1950s.'

Margaret glanced around at attentive faces. Quite a trick to pull people off the street, out of their hectic worries, and involve them in the world of imagination and spirit. He was good at knowing what people needed, like a woman in that respect, she thought. He closed the door on petty irritations for an hour and drew each person into his loving arms.

'Miller has a bold conscience which exposes bitterness and self-righteousness. He distills issues into moral questions, implying that we each must make individual choices.'

The coat in the plastic Watson's Cleaners bag slipped off the seat, crumbling to the floor with the sound of electricity crackling down a telephone pole in the rain. Several people turned. Roger Bentman stretched his neck slightly, surveying the back pew. Mortified, Margaret ducked down and retrieved the coat, securing it on the seat with her purse. Bentman continued calmly, as if Mount Vesuvius had not just erupted.

'So Miller is writing about the courage to see the world clearly as well as about the courage to act in it. This is an integrity of vision.'

Margaret was surprised when the talk ended. Was it one o'clock already − time to climb back up the hill?

At the door, he shook hands warmly, remembering everyone's name, asking personal questions. Margaret was surprised when he reached over for her arm, inquiring if she might stay behind for a moment. She didn't have to rush back to the shop, did she? Of course he would know that. Of course he would remember.

Finally the vestibule cleared, except for them and Slocum sleeping under the literature table.

'Do you like *The Crucible*?' he inquired.

'Oh, yes, your talk was lovely,' she faltered. It was so

much more than lovely. Powerful, profound, but these words did not come readily. 'I learned a great deal today.'

'The play,' he asked, 'have you seen it?'

She hated appearing stupid. Usually she could get away with what Rob called 'bullshitting' unless someone asked a direct question like this.

'No,' she sighed. 'I've never seen it. There's so much I haven't seen.'

'Good, good,' Bentman was saying.

He studied her worried face and, not knowing what to make of it, he spoke more rapidly. 'I've just received two tickets to the production at the Geary Theatre. I was hoping you might join me.'

'Oh, yes,' Margaret blushed deeper with each breath. 'I mean I'd love to go. That would be lovely.' Lovely. Damn, she would go home and look up synonyms for lovely. She resolved not to say the word for an entire year.

'Fine,' Bentman clasped her hand. 'I'm very pleased.'

Nine

Chrissie and Margaret had been talking about their trip to Golden Gate Park for a week. As soon as they sat beside each other on the Muni bus, silence dropped heavily between them. Chrissie, frustrated by her five failed attempts at conversation, stared out the bus window.

Margaret seemed to be engrossed in her lap. She was convincing herself that she needn't tell Chrissie about her date. Perhaps she and the Reverend would go out once and that would be that. Besides, Chrissie couldn't monitor every second of her life. It wasn't as though Chrissie had wanted to spend the evening with her. She had been nattering on about some kind of testimonial dinner for Marissa Washington.

'You in a slump or something?' Chrissie turned back to her friend. 'You seem tired, or tense.'

'Oh, no, just . . .' Margaret considered blaming her mood on the recent muggings on the Muni. That would just get Chrissie raving about the election. The trouble with knowing someone so well is that they could tell when you were being evasive just from the way you sat or breathed.

Margaret decided to lie. 'I got another letter from Janey.' She inhaled slowly, giving herself time to find the next words. 'And I worry about her in those cold Canadian winters.'

'In October?' Chrissie asked. Why hadn't Margaret shown her the letter? She always shared Janey's letters.

'An early cold wave,' Margaret said uncertainly. 'They get quite a lot of snow in British Columbia.'

'What are you going on about?' asked Chrissie. 'You lived over half your life in that savage New York weather. You survived. You're always fretting about Rob in Alaska and Janey in Canada. They know where to buy coats and gloves and boots. Leave them alone.'

'You're right.' Margaret looked past Chrissie, out the bus window at the clouds threatening their afternoon. 'I'm such a fussbudget.'

Chrissie tried to lighten the mood. 'Aye, I've always thought Janey took more after me.'

Margaret smiled.

'The ideal tomboy, I was. With six footballers in the family, it was either run or get smashed.'

'You're pretty tough.' Margaret shook her head. 'Tougher than your brothers, I guess. You must have had something special to be able to leave Scotland, to emigrate *alone* to America.' Margaret paused, disconcerted by this unfamiliar terrain. They rarely discussed Chrissie's life. 'Wasn't it a hard choice?' she pursued cautiously.

'No choice, really,' said Chrissie. She lapsed into the cloudy grey sky and felt comforted by this color of her childhood. She wondered if it were worth answering Margaret, worth cutting through her friend's romance about Scotland to describe the prejudices and pomposity of Edinburgh the Good. How much should she try to explain? How much disappointment should she risk? Finally she said, 'The Bloody Queen.'

'Pardon?' Margaret wondered if Chrissie were being sarcastic, drawing down the blind again.

'The King in those days,' continued Chrissie, still watching the city pass behind them. 'I remember the day I decided to leave. His Majesty was in Edinburgh, at Holyrood House, doing something relevant for the national welfare like grouse shooting. He took a ceremonial ride down the Royal Mile.'

Margaret tried to imagine Chrissie's steel wool hair returned to auburn curls around a firey young face.

'And do you know what was worse than his pretentiousness?' demanded Chrissie. 'I was just fifteen or sixteen at the time, but I'll never forget it. What was worse was the shopkeepers. The same ones who were always complaining about their taxes going to his fancy houses and lavish dinners and gilded chariots. The shopkeepers and folks in the street all stopped to gawk at him. Some of them clapped. For the bloody *King of England.* Some of them cheered! I couldn't believe it. I couldn't comprehend the hypocrisy and stupidity.' Chrissie was still distracted, staring out at Market Street.

Margaret leaned over, trying to catch her friend's reflection in the bus window.

'I remember spitting on the pavement in front of MacRae's Dairy and heading straight off to the library to find a country with no kings or kowtowing shopkeepers. Australia was my first thought. But they still had the Union Jack in their flag and I heard that when the King made a trip to Melbourne the same hoo-ha went on there. So I picked America. Someday I would go to America.'

'You've never told me this,' said Margaret. 'It's like a history book. How come you never told me?'

Chrissie looked puzzled and finally turned to Margaret. 'Maybe I had to wait for the right time.'

'Thirty years?' asked Margaret.

'Are you scolding me?' Chrissie raised one nest of an eyebrow.

'Maybe a little,' said Margaret.

'Hmmm.' Chrissie stared across the aisle, at nothing, at Rajid. Yes, she should tell Margaret the awful story of Rajid; she should face it again, herself.

'Well, maybe you're right about Janey.' Margaret resumed the more comfortable subject. 'Maybe she's just more independent than I ever was. I mean, for years after Mom's death I felt tied to her, still missed her.'

'Margaret, *why* are you always so self-effacing? Independence doesn't mean you can't miss someone. Don't you think I miss Scotland, for all its soot and poverty? Don't you think I miss long summer nights and the security of a coal fire during a dark February afternoon? Don't you think I miss the rows with James, Alex and the others? I was so tied to it I thought I would never find myself. Listen, I'm not comfortable talking in grand psychological abstraction like this.'

Margaret nodded, reflecting that Chrissie was comfortable with psychology as a political tool, as a way of understanding public motivation. But when the psychology got personal, Chrissie grew scared and called it 'abstraction'.

'Maybe the reason Rob and Janey moved so far away is that they love you,' said Chrissie, ignoring a twitch of jealousy in her stomach.

'That makes no sense.'

'They both love you, Margaret,' Chrissie exclaimed. 'Rob is always calling or sending presents. And Janey! Why you're

61

the bloody heroine of her poems. She sends letters every couple of weeks. Or maybe more.' Her blue eyes flattened with her voice. 'Maybe I don't get informed how often.'

'No,' Margaret protested.

'She needs a life of her own,' declared Chrissie.

'So far away?'

'Margaret, love, she's *not* so far away.' Chrissie's tone hardened when she was trying to be clear. 'Not far away compared to *us* from *our mothers.* You and Janey are lucky to have each other at your ages. Now,' she put up her hand, 'don't fuss. I'm not calling you an old woman, but you and I both lost our mothers when we were girls. You and Janey have each other. That's progress.'

Margaret shrugged. She didn't feel like arguing. And they had finally reached the park. The dark sky chilled her as they climbed off the bus. With a little luck it would stay dry through their walk to the Tea Garden. She regarded Chrissie's set expression and felt somewhat awed that they had ever become friends.

'Well, Lady Christine,' said Margaret, craning her neck to address her companion who was a stately six inches taller. 'I hope our colonial park suits your noble taste. I, myself, have entertained many a royal here, but none so honorable as yourself.'

'The one thing I've always said about you,' laughed Chrissie, 'is that you know how to deal with aristocrats.'

By the time they reached the Tea Garden, Margaret had resolved to conceal her date from Chrissie. And within minutes of sitting down, Chrissie asked about Reverend Bentman. Truly, there was a witch in that woman. Margaret had always wondered about those eyes, yes, cat's eyes. Pop had told her about such eyes which changed with the light, as if they might see under and through anything at all.

'He's fine,' said Margaret, suddenly absorbed in cracking her fortune cookie. The darn thing wouldn't break, no matter where she pressed.

'You're in fine shape today.' Chrissie pulled a face.

Margaret stared at her trembling fingers.

'So what's going on with you two anyway?' Chrissie immediately regretted the question for, in some ways, she did not want to know.

'Just because someone asks you to a play doesn't mean that you're going to get married,' Margaret blurted, cracking the cookie with the end of her sentence.

'Marriage,' said Chrissie, a quick toughness masking her alarm. 'Who's talking about marriage?'

' "Prosperity," ' Margaret read in a thin voice. 'It says "Prosperity will come soon. Money will pass through your hands." Now how do they know I work at a cash register?'

'Fortune cookies are more profound.' Chrissie tried not to hear the edge in her voice. 'That means *real* prosperity. Your *own* money. Maybe you and the good Reverend will rip off the poor box and escape together to Monte Carlo.'

'Chrissie,' Margaret snapped loudly enough to attract attention from the couple seated on the next bench. 'What's got into you?'

She watched Chrissie blush, if it could be called blushing. So controlled was Chrissie that her only visible sign of distress was a sliver of pink crossing her forehead.

'What's wrong with spending a little time with Reverend Bentman?' Margaret asked. She wanted to say how nervous she felt. Why had he chosen *her* to escort to the theatre? Perhaps she was his charity case for the week. She would not be smart enough for him. She would be a terrible disappointment.

'Such a milktoast.' Chrissie paused, momentarily wondering if she were jealous that Bentman had Margaret or that Margaret had someone interested in her. Regardless, she decided, her objections were sound. 'Such a wet noodle.'

'What do you mean?' Margaret flared and munched loudly on the cookie as Chrissie replied.

'Look at the election.'

'No, I'm tired of the election,' Margaret was furious. 'We're talking about a man, not about politics!'

'You can tell a lot about a man from the way he responds to a difficult situation,' said Chrissie. 'And Robber — Roger Bentman has been wishy-washy on the election. Marissa stands for all he's preached about "downtown community".'

'What's your point?' Margaret chafed under Chrissie's self-righteousness.

'My point —' Chrissie interrupted herself, waving for the

63

Japanese waitress, 'Check please,' she called before the woman reached their table.

They each watched with sympathy as the waitress in her tight kimono waddled like a drydocked mermaid back to her desk.

'My point,' Chrissie finished, 'is that he won't do a thing to help her.'

'Perhaps you've never heard of the separation between Church and State.' Margaret was sorry she had acquired Chrissie's sarcastic tone.

'Don't give me civics lessons,' exploded Chrissie. 'I'm a naturalized citizen. We're even more pious than those born into the fold. I know the difference between preaching politics and preaching morality.'

How much she sounded like Douglas Sinclair, thought Margaret. Clearly the two of them would agree about Reverend Bentman as well as about the election.

'He's a good man,' Margaret said unsteadily. She wanted not to cry. She wanted not to shout. She concentrated on the words. 'He doesn't believe it's appropriate to get mixed up in it.'

'A sacred man,' agreed Chrissie, 'can't afford to get "mixed up".'

The waitress, in a moment of superbly orchestrated tact, appeared with the bill. As she left, the old silence settled coolly between them. They each checked the addition, then pulled money, including generous tips, from their purses.

'When it comes to the tip,' Chrissie said, surprised at her conciliatory tone, 'you can always count on other waitresses.'

Ten

Ernie, hunched over his coffee mug in a back booth, faced the nearly empty café. Chrissie rested her legs on the seat and stared at the crowds passing under the four o'clock shadows of oversized buildings. Now that the election was closing in, Ernie dropped by almost every day for a coffee break. This afternoon their strategy meeting was continually disrupted by Chrissie's irritability.

'Margaret has no sense of the real world,' said Chrissie, straightening the dark seam in her support hose. 'You'd think she was Marie Antoinette, the amount she cares about the costs of transport and food. Besides, the company she keeps!'

'I'd hardly call Roger Bentman Louis XVI,' laughed Ernie. 'Don't you think you're getting a little carried away?'

'Carried away,' she barked. 'Margaret's the one who's getting carried away. "Get me to the church on time . . ." '

'I've never heard that rendered with a Scottish brogue before,' said Ernie. Failing to raise a smile, he added, 'What's going on? Doesn't Margaret deserve a little romance, a little fun?'

'Hmmm.' Chrissie sniffed and could not fail to wonder at the tightness in her throat. She hated being so emotional because she knew it had as much to do with her loneliness as with Margaret's poor judgment. 'I suppose you think that's all there is to life — sex and sweet words and other distractions.'

'*Who*'s distracted? I came here for a strategy meeting. You're the one changing the topic.'

Chrissie ignored him, caught up in a scene from earlier that day — Bernie waving over a taxi driver. The exchange of money was visible if you watched closely, if you knew what to look for. Bernie reaching into the cab with a piece of paper supposedly giving directions. The driver slipped a fiver into Bernie's white glove. Bernie nodding, satisfied, and ushering the guests into the taxi with one hand, depositing the money with the other into his deep pocket. This sort of incident would pass Margaret by completely, although she lived in the same neighborhood. She would be so shocked that sweet Bernie, who remembered her with those goddamned flowers on her birthday, could be dishonest. She might even try to return the flowers. How had Margaret survived as a young kid taking care of a younger one in New York? Such naïvety! Margaret had no idea how cities worked. Maybe that's why she had survived.

'You still with me?' asked Ernie. 'Or have you taken up transcendental meditation?'

'You've got to admit,' Chrissie surfaced, 'that Bentman is a real problem. Fuzzy liberals cloud the issues by insisting on "fairness". What's fair about Carson and his speculator thugs buying up buildings and raising the rents? If they had their way, they'd turn the Tenderloin into one vast Ramada-Holiday-Hilton Hotel.' She knew she sounded rhetorical, that Ernie didn't need the lecture. Still, it settled her to repeat the details. Reciting facts, like brisk exercise, made her easier. 'What's fair about devastating the neighborhood?'

'Bourgeois revisionist pig.' Ernie suppressed a smile, recalling Roberto's subtle epithet about the Reverend.

'You're not taking this seriously!' She checked her watch, only ten more minutes of the break. Why was she wasting it camping around with Ernie?

'Sure I am,' he said. 'Here at your service: Ernie Parenti, BA Philosophy, San Francisco State University, flower peddler extraordinaire, gay activist, downtown citizen. Speaking of which, I think I've captured that bar over in the Castro for a benefit next week. Could rake in a few thou.'

'We'll need more than that,' Chrissie was purposeful again, 'after the speech Carson gave at the Bosworth Club, after all his free publicity.'

'And after you finish paying for a new headquarters.'

Chrissie turned to the anxious voice behind her.

Douglas Sinclair's face was drained of color except for inflammation around his eye sockets.

'Marissa's headquarters,' he stopped, for breath, or perhaps in some futile hope of contradiction. 'Her headquarters got firebombed thirty minutes ago.'

Chrissie stared, wanting it to be untrue, yet needing him to explain.

'Three-thirty.' Douglas spoke more rapidly, impersonal as a teletype. 'No one hurt. Everything gutted. All records destroyed. No immediate suspects.'

Chrissie remained silent, her broad back clenched into the stillness of a boulder. She was too stunned to be surprised by her own silence. Stunned by a torrent of memories from fifty years before. Silence. Blood. Rocks. Rocks pelting against Rajid's body. Rocks bouncing off the North Bridge to the roadway below. Laughter, spitting, slapping, kicking. Silence. Silence from her mouth as they held her against the wall, wog whore. Her mouth opened to scream and nothing, silence. Nothing but fear and astonishment and hate and shame and nothing. Nothing. Nothing could be done. The doctors tried. Worked all night at the Royal Infirmary. But his kidneys gave out. Boots in the kidneys. Honest workmen's boots. He never recovered consciousness. They never recovered the gang. Did the gang ever recover conscience? Impossible to recognize behind the masks. Their swift feet clopped across the cobble stones faster than the police horses could follow. Of course, evil men are faster than white horses. Later she was advised not to prosecute. What was the point? What was the evidence? What were the grounds? Ground. They buried him quietly in that cold northern ground so far from Delhi. James and herself and a young Indian minister who didn't know Rajid, didn't know his religion. So for a prayer, they had passed a moment's silence.

'Dirty bastards,' Chrissie heard her own voice. She grabbed Sinclair's hand for strength and then released it. 'No immediate suspects,' she repeated angrily. 'Do they think the Viet Cong did it?'

Now Ernie and Douglas were silent.

'So where were Carson's louts during this? I suppose they have alibis. Collecting rent, perhaps? Carson was probably drinking tea with the Archbishop! We'll get them. We'll haul them into court.'

Ernie stirred his coffee grounds, staring absently across the café. 'To think it really happened. What we've been talking about. Like back in the sixties when we were paranoid that they were tapping our phones. And it turned out that they really were.'

The color was returning to Douglas's face. 'Well, it *really* happened,' he whispered sourly.

'God.' Ernie scraped the spoon back and forth, back and forth. 'To think that people in your own neighborhood could do a thing like that.'

Douglas's cheeks were a high red now. 'Or people in your own family.'

Chrissie didn't hear them. She thought about that afternoon alone in the office when she had been frightened away by the ping, ping of rain. She thought about her files on Carson's accounts. How could she pull all that information together again?

'You can't be talking about Kevin.' Ernie dropped his spoon against the side of the cup. 'He's not the type. Why he's not even . . .'

'Smart enough?' said Douglas.

'No,' reluctantly, 'gutsy enough.'

'Not for planting bombs, maybe,' shot Douglas, 'but he's connected somehow.'

'Listen, man.' Ernie tentatively put his hand on Sinclair's arm. He had learned to be guarded in his friendship with straight men in order to obviate double messages. 'Don't get over-heated. Kevin's politics are a little − weird − but I don't think he'd go to such extremes.' Ernie looked to Chrissie for corroboration.

She shrugged and read her watch. 'Ernie, it'll be another two hours till I get down there. Will you see what's happening? Tell them I'll come as soon as I'm off work?'

'Sure, sweet,' he said, dropping a dollar on the table for coffee.

Douglas followed him out the door.

Sweet, the word curdled on her tongue. In the land of milk and honey you had to beware of sweets, had to check what they were laced with. Curiously, Chrissie felt a stillness, a cleanness. This firebombing could be a turning point. Threats of violence were one thing. Rocks were another. But a building destroyed − thank God not a life − this could change the Tenderloin. Would Marissa give up? Would Carson be discovered? How could he manage to stay clear of charges? He was behind it all, wasn't he? A bombing would bring change, yet what change?

Her station was empty except for two tables. Chrissie wished she were busier, to keep her mind off the fire. Old Mrs Douglas was eating her usual afternoon layercake. A married couple from Atlanta were starting dinner. Dinner at 4 pm. You got odd orders when you worked with jet-lagged customers. And odd behavior. Of course Margaret was right that she preferred this type to the street people who couldn't remember what they ordered and, often as not, couldn't pay for it.

Helen Reddy was belting out 'Delta Dawn'. Why did all the singers sound the same on Muzak?

The fire. Her mind wandered again. No, no use worrying until she could investigate for herself. How she hated slow days. She enjoyed working on top form; enjoyed serving people decent meals — on time, piping hot. Since lukewarm soup was one of her personal peeves, she was especially careful with the soup. Two tables today. Only two. Damn. Usually on slow days she hung out at the order rack chatting with the other girls. Or she tried to catch Margaret's eye in the news shop across the street. Today she couldn't bear to see Margaret, so she just leaned on the counter and waited.

Chrissie tried to imagine how the papers would report the firebombing, but her mind kept skipping back to Margaret. Why was she throwing herself on this namby-pamby priest? God, she'd taken up with the strangest assortment of men over the years. That bank manager from the Sunset District who raised Siamese cats. The Czechoslovakian refugee who worked in the *Examiner* print shop and claimed to be a great sculptor. And George Lemington III, the salesman from Seattle who promised to whisk her off to the Land of Evergreen. Margaret took care of each man until it was time for him to move on. All very well to buy a few dinners and roll in the hay, but none of them wanted to adopt three children. Each one left after she gave him all she had. Then she would return to Chrissie. Why didn't Margaret learn? Reverend Roger Bentman, blandest of the bland. You'd think a woman would realize something by the time she made seventy. You'd think she could be satisfied with loyal friends.

'Meeting tonight,' Ernie stuck his head round the door, shouting over the customers from Atlanta. 'Seven pm at Glide. I told them you'd be there.'

'Thanks.' She waved her pencil. 'See you then.'

Watching Ernie hurry down Geary Street, she saw a slightly aging version of the suave young man who became her friend fifteen years before because they were both addicted to the 'Carry On' movies from London. At forty, he still had the same conscious swagger of the hips, the same swan-arched neck, the same shiny hair — or, if not the same shiny hair, at least it was dyed the same shiny blue-black shade. Apparently he used Margaret's brand of henna. That was one thing she didn't understand about gay men. Why did they pick the worst things about women to imitate?

Aye, he was much better than in the old days. Steadier. Voice clearer. Eyes more focused. Then he had been on so many medications he couldn't remember all the names. Doing so many things he couldn't remember what was next. Going to school part-time; selling flowers part-time. So many parts. The drugs, he insisted, were better than the electric shock treatment his parents in Kirkland, Washington had insisted upon when he announced he was gay. He had told her during the intermission to one of those silly movies that it had taken him six months to get out of the hospital. And another six months to get his head together and find a bus to San Francisco.

Where was her mind trailing today? Perhaps she couldn't cope with the enormity of the fire. Regardless, she'd better start coping with this job. Mr M could easily find a replacement. The union rep from Local Two had lost a case just last week.

Chrissie walked round her tables. Mrs Dougal was doing fine with the cake, eating the frosting first, because, as she explained to Chrissie often enough, the frosting was the best part and she didn't want to get full before she ate it. A little crazy, Mrs Dougal, but in a thoroughly logical way. The man from Atlanta looked up. 'Ketchup, please.' 'Mustard, please.' 'More cream, please.' She nodded in a distant, courteous manner and answered his needs.

Resting back against the wall, she imagined Ernie on that bus to San Francisco. But why San Francisco? Why had they all chosen San Francisco? Ernie on the Greyhound bus, carrying a knapsack of t-shirts and denim and a paperback collection of Rilke. Margaret driving cross-country in a broken-down Buick with Bill and their three kids. Herself on the transcontinental train with an old canvas suitcase 'loaned' by James. He knew she would come back. Now, she wondered, had he ever needed it? He had promised to visit her a dozen times, just as frequently as she had promised to come home.

'More coffee, please.' The man from Atlanta. 'She'll have tea.'

Why didn't the woman speak for herself; Chrissie was tempted to ask if she were dumb. Instead, she nodded, returning with hot coffee and tea.

'Thank you,' he said.

'Thank you, darling,' she said.

So cordial these Southern customers, a little too sugary for her taste. But her taste didn't count. It was their dinner. And Southerners were big tippers if you served them right. Lavish, but generally insincere, thought Chrissie. Margaret said she made too many generalizations and that you couldn't judge a book by its cover. Chrissie said she didn't have time for browsing.

She knew why *she* had come to San Francisco. It was simple, almost predictable. She had come for the American dream. She left her waitressing job at Stuart's Café on Castle Street in search of roads paved with . . . who knows? At least they would be paved. (They wouldn't be made of cobblestones which could be dug up and hurled at a poor immigrant. Not in America. They wanted strangers here. They had built their country on the backs of immigrants. Polish Americans. Chinese Americans. German Americans. Even WASPS like herself, although this was a loathsome identity nowadays. She supposed she could call herself a Celt instead.) So she went from Stuart's Café to Mummer's Café. Some dream. Recurring nightmare. She wrote imaginary letters to the divine arbiter and then revised them. Well, this did make a change of scene.

A rap on the window. She looked up. Roberto. Fist in the

air, he was running down toward headquarters. Seven o'clock, she remembered and held up seven fingers for their meeting tonight. He nodded and shook his fist again. As he passed out of sight, she checked her watch. Just 5 pm. This couple were still nibbling their Goldrush Pineapple Cake.

'Coffee, Miss,' the man called abruptly. What he didn't say was, You've got only two tables, why can't you pay more attention? What she didn't say was, I'm old enough to be your grandmother, buster, so hold your horses. She refilled his cup.

'My Aunt From California,' that was the name of the play that had drawn her here. She had read it in the sixth or seventh grade. They didn't call it sixth or seventh grade in Scotland. How could she forget that? She hated when her fuzzy memory made her feel old. She didn't mind being a senior citizen. Didn't mind the getting of wisdom. But how soon was that followed by the getting of senility? Douglas Sinclair had recommended Vitamin C. Although she didn't believe in artificial stimuli — with the exception of a brandy here and there — she did stock up on Vitamin C at the last Walgreen's sale.

Leaning back against the counter, she thought how Margaret had loved working at the Cornucopia Restaurant and how she herself had hated New York. You would have thought she was a stockyard animal the way they had inspected her for fleas, pounded her chest in search of tuberculosis, almost turned her upside down to guarantee she wasn't a prostitute. No, she didn't like New York. Didn't like the squeezed accents in which they asked their nasty questions. So she took the train as far away as possible and wound up in San Francisco. James and the other boys enjoyed her letters, said California sounded very interesting, but they wished there weren't so many foreign Papist names, 'San' this and 'San' that. She told them they'd love the sun on the palm trees in January. They'd have a real lark when they came. They didn't come. After a period, the letters dwindled. James was the only one who continued to write faithfully at Christmas. And that last letter — the one from Jenny about his stroke — was seven, eight months ago.

'Check, Miss,' the gentleman called a little too loudly.

Chrissie nodded, holding her ground a moment, as if the customer had just interrupted her crucial ruminations on next week's menu or the cook's timetable. Never lose your dignity, Miss Stuart had taught her. Waitressing is a job, just like theirs, only probably more honest.

Eleven

Saturday night arrived far too soon for Margaret. Six o'clock already and she was still in her ragged blue chenille robe wondering what to wear. The peach shirtwaist or the navy trouser suit? The nicest clothes she owned. Each of a different order, a different mood. Flaring out the skirt of the dress, she thought she favored it, a very feminine frock which brought out the pinks in her skin. Yes, she still had nice skin ('Her best point,' Mom would say. 'No, that's her mind,' Pop would argue, 'an intelligent girl, our daughter.') Hmmm, such an intelligent girl that sixty years later she couldn't decide what to wear. The trouser suit was dignified, tailored and quite chic with these shoulder pads. However she had worn it to Russell Foster's funeral and she wondered if Roger would remember.

Margaret laid both garments on a chair and paced across the living-room. Slocum sat in her favorite corner of the couch, guarding Margaret's nervousness. From the window, Margaret tried to spot Chrissie, who would be going to work now since she was taking an extra shift for Jeannette whose mother was sick up in Chico.

She wished she were going out with Chrissie tonight, to one of her silly British movies or down to the Edinburgh Castle for that whining music and warm beer.

'Old pal, how did I get myself into this mess?'

Slocum climbed down from the couch — a manoeuvre she used to accomplish in one hop but which now required three or four lumbering movements — and walked over to Margaret. She sniffed around Margaret's ankles. Then finding the perfect spot on the right foot, she began to lick. Margaret wondered whether Slocum distinguished people by their feet the way she recognized them by their faces.

She turned slightly and found her drawn face in Grandma's mirror, looking for all the world as if she didn't have a single friend beside this splendid dog. The problem was that she missed Chrissie. Missed Chrissie telling her what to wear, telling her everything would be all right.

Chrissie had been distracted all week over this wretched firebombing. For several days, she had been certain they would lock up Jake Carson. Then the explosion was tied to a drug gang. The police said a man was dealing heroin in the next office and that Marissa's headquarters had been 'an incidental casualty.'

Margaret remembered how Chrissie spent the next couple of days acting angrier than ever, outraged that the police had conspired to protect Carson. Margaret just didn't know who was right. Perhaps Carson could do a thing like that. Perhaps. Chrissie was as unpredictable as one of those delayed fire-crackers. Anything might set her off. Margaret tried to keep her friend out of the shop whenever she thought Kevin might be coming through.

The explosion not only destroyed Marissa's headquarters, Margaret learned, it created aftershocks all over town. Picketing, editorials, street fights. She thought that politics was an awfully inhumane process for something that was supposed to serve humanity. 'Broken windows,' as Marissa had said that night at Glide. 'Broken arm . . .' Margaret reached down and stroked Slocum's soft head. She would write to Janey about all this. It helped to write down her worries. It made them clearer. Made her feel less alone.

Not that she was really alone. Not with a friend like Chrissie. It was just that she had to be careful about certain topics. Certain people. Such as Kevin. Why was Chrissie so critical, so ungiving? Margaret suspected her friend disliked the fellow as much for his weakness as for any wrong-doing. Chrissie, in her Scots' strength, would never allow dear Kevin an inch. Wouldn't even credit the lad for being generous — with the flowers he brought her, these presents for his sick teacher. Kevin was always so shy in his ways of giving, so modest. Sinclair didn't even know what a gentleman he had raised.

The other person they rarely discussed was Roger Bentman. Lately, Margaret realized, it had been she herself who didn't wish to talk, who changed the topic. Ever since Chrissie had found out about this 'date' with Bentman, there was no end to her sniping about 'middle class religion'.

Margaret held up the navy trouser suit and approached the mirror. Too grim. She wanted to be cheerful tonight. Chrissie be damned. No, how awful to have such thoughts about an old friend who had, after all, helped her pick out the peach dress at Magnarama last spring.

The dome clock on her dresser chimed 6:30. Startled, she surveyed the studio apartment: afghan tossed over the chair, box of graham crackers on the coffee table, Slocum's dried food scattered on the kitchen floor by the bowl. And she hadn't even started cleaning the bathroom. Why didn't she just accept his invitation to go out to the St Francis for a drink? No, no, that wasn't Margaret's style. She couldn't take too much generosity. For heaven's sake, he was providing the theatre tickets. At least she could reciprocate with a cocktail. The theatre was so close. Now, as she swept up after Slocum, she froze with the broom in her hand. Wouldn't it be terrible if he ran into Chrissie in the lobby. Paralyzed for a moment, Margaret stared blankly at the green kitchen wall, then scolded herself — all this worrying was ridiculous and egotistical too.

He arrived at 7:15, jot on time, as Chrissie would say. With flowers, a lovely bouquet of yellow daisies and white roses. Margaret thanked him profusely, holding them as far from her troublesome nose as possible. Chrissie's favorite colors, what a pity they had come from Bentman. Still, her neighbor, Mrs Winchester, would be pleased with the bouquet. She placed it in a cut glass vase — her only vase because no sooner did flowers arrive than they departed — and set the vase next to the domed clock.

'What a splendid clock.' Bentman was on his feet again, revealing a nervousness that Margaret had never noticed in the shop or the pulpit. 'Wherever did you find such an antique?'

'The girls at Mummer's, when I left,' she said, handing him a martini. 'I was always fascinated by these things as a kid. Pop had a customer who repaired them. So a good friend of mine' (she would not mention Chrissie by name, would not invite her hex) 'organized the buying of it as a farewell gift.'

'Lovely taste,' he said, surveying the rest of the room

quickly, his eyes pausing only on Janey's Degas print.

When he sat down, the room seemed larger to Margaret, and filled with a vast silence.

'These pictures,' he was on his feet again, examining the sepia portraits of her parents and an enlarged color snapshot of the three children. 'What a handsome family, past and present. Your father.' He looked back at her. 'You look a lot like your father.'

'Yes,' Margaret spoke stiffly. She gulped the martini and almost immediately felt it rise to her head, clearing away good sense and leaving her breathing in an oxygenless atmosphere. Quickly she took a potato chip and filled it with creamy onion dip. 'So who do you look like?' she managed to say, before stuffing the salty ballast down her throat.

He seemed puzzled.

She noticed he hadn't touched the potato chips. Probably not the class of hors d'oeuvre he was used to. Empty calories, as Janey would say. But Margaret didn't know how to cope with fancier food like caviar and fondue. He wasn't touching the martini, either. Not more than a sip. Was something wrong with it? Nice gin, Giorgio at the grocery had told her. Five dollars for a small bottle and he had given it to Margaret for $3.50. An off-brand or something? No, Giorgio wouldn't cheat Margaret. Maybe the tourists, but not Margaret. She had known him since he was a boy. Perhaps the Reverend preferred wine. Red wine. Blood of Christ and all that. No, no, not for a Unitarian. What was she doing, thinking about?

He still look confused.

'Which member of your family,' she tried to clarify, having eaten another potato chip in hopes that it might anchor her to the chair, 'do you resemble?'

'Well,' he smiled to himself. 'I'd like to say it was my father.' Bentman smiled more broadly. ' "Mr Adonis" his fraternity brothers called him. However, I'm afraid I look a lot more like Uncle Arthur, who was better known for his golf game than his beauty.'

'Not at all,' said Margaret, her attention unaccountably drawn to a speck of fluff on his blue tweed sleeve. Nice cloth, she thought. Pop often said he would have liked to be a draper if he'd been able to get an apprenticeship.

77

A siren wailed up Geary Street. Enough distraction to admit a new topic.

'So tell me how your daughter is doing?' he asked. 'I read that article in *Time* last month. Another book out, eh?'

'Yes,' blushed Margaret, hoping he wouldn't ask to see it, embarrassed by the erotic poems, some of them about women, one of them unspeakably like herself.

'I read the poems with great interest,' Bentman began.

'You read them?' She tried, too late, to hide her astonishment.

'Oh, yes.' He spoke thoughtfully. 'Real progress in form. Mind you, I also liked the first two volumes. Florence greatly admired the second book. My wife taught poetry, you know.'

Margaret nodded, still amazed that someone she knew followed Janey's work. That kind of fancy sensual writing was a little like pornography, she had reckoned, and no one she knew was likely to stumble across it. At the mention of his wife's name, Margaret watched him for traces of sadness. Just a bit of narrowing in the eyes. Chrissie always said Florence Bentman was a snob. Margaret had defended her as shy.

'You must be proud,' he was saying. 'It isn't everyone who has a poet in the family.'

For some peculiar reason, Margaret wanted to tell him that she, herself, was also a writer, that Mrs Johnson had compared her to Lady Gregory, that she still watched the world closely, as if she might write about it. Instead, she deposited another potato chip in her mouth. Better to sober up.

'I particularly liked the fox sequence in the last book,' Bentman continued.

Was this to cover up the silence? she wondered. Had he noticed her silence?

'Yes,' Margaret said. 'To tell you the truth, I don't completely understand all her poems.' Why was she telling him the truth? She decided to sit back a while and let him talk.

He noticed her discomfort and changed the topic again, 'Your son Rob, he likes the fishing business?'

Nodding, Margaret regarded Rob in the picture. Tall, skinny, worried. The same serious look he wore the day he was born. Responsibility of being the oldest, perhaps. Or the

heart valve. They had fretted so when he g⸻
when the doctor said he'd have heart murmurs⸻
his life. She could hear them murmuring now⸻
mother, terrible mother. How could she know the⸻
murmuring would keep him from Vietnam, from ⸻ ₋₋le
that would kill her perfect, happy baby Michael. But ₋₋oger
hadn't asked about Michael. He had asked about Rob. She
loved Rob, although somehow she didn't know him as well
as the others.

'He likes the sea,' answered Margaret. 'He likes to be free,
on the move, to visit strange places. Even on vacation, he
takes a backpack and goes hiking to the tundra. Such a
cold place, Alaska, I'll never understand it. He's happy. No,
maybe "happy" isn't the right word. Rob doesn't have the
temperament to feel happy. He's content. Well, satisfied.'

'I like the way you try for precision,' he said. 'That's a
special kind of honesty.'

She watched his smile and saw that he liked her very much
indeed. For the first time this evening, she could imagine
reasons why. She *was* an attractive woman, kind, bright,
precise. Margaret appreciated that he appreciated her precision.
Finally, she said, 'Thank you.'

His patient grey eyes waited for her to continue. Lord, she
had been blathering on. Served her right. Never could handle
alcohol. Chrissie would always drink her under the table. It
was one thing to be tipsy with her pal and quite another to
be foolish in front of the Reverend.

'You had no children?' Not really a question, however she
needed to deflect the focus, to catch her breath, to hear
him talk.

'No,' he said, the smile gone now. 'Florence and I had to
parent in other ways. We raised a foster son for three years.
Then, clearly, there were the parish children.'

'Clearly.' Margaret ruffled the warm fur around Slocum's
neck. The dog had been sullen ever since their guest arrived.
Usually she was all over visitors. Tonight she just stuck close
to Margaret's feet in a watchful slump.

'Florence reached out in many ways. Her teaching at the
Senior Center, for instance. She didn't actually have the
sensibility for children. Rather too finely tuned.'

Was she finely tuned enough to be Lady Gregory? wondered Margaret. Perhaps Bentman thought that she herself was different, of sturdier stock. If he couldn't see that she was also finely tuned, why was he taking her to this fancy play? Her hands were shaking. What had got into her? She had to stop this scene spinning in her head. She considered slipping into the kitchen for a cup of instant coffee.

'Well,' Bentman said cheerfully, 'if we're going to spend the evening with Arthur Miller, we'd better get moving.'

Arthur Miller, she thought. He probably doesn't think I know who Arthur Miller is. 'I really enjoyed *Death of a Salesman*,' said Margaret, who had passed an afternoon at the library that week, 'much better than *After the Fall*'.

'Yes,' Bentman looked around for his coat. 'I agree.' There was no surprise in his voice. Perhaps he knew all about Lady Gregory.

The foyer of the Geary Theatre was packed. Margaret felt calmer after their brisk walk. As she surveyed the fashions, she was glad she had worn the peach dress.

Mr Poulos, in his Saturday night best brown suit, nodded to her from over by the ticket booth, craning his neck to determine her companion. When he noticed, he nodded again, with a smile of approval that made her uncomfortable. She could just imagine him gossiping with Mrs Dougal and Mr Gleason. No, she wouldn't get caught in conceit. She would concentrate on the play and on Roger Bentman.

He was talking to her.

'Beg pardon,' she said, blushing vividly. She could see the rosiness all the way down her fingers.

Concentrate. She must concentrate. If he hadn't already pegged her for a lush, he would decide she was senile.

'Isn't that Jake Carson over there?' he asked quietly.

She recognized the man from under the hat, the man from the television debate. Next to him stood Kevin, in a sharp, checked suit which was just a bit tight around the thighs.

'And young Sinclair,' Bentman continued. 'I didn't know the two of them were friends.'

Unsure if she would betray Kevin by acknowledging the acquaintance, Margaret responded, 'Kevin takes an active interest in the development of the downtown community.'

'As a real estate agent, I suspect he would,' Bentman said tersely.

Before Margaret had a chance to interpret his tone, the lobby lights blinked. Blackout, she tasted a tip of panic. The theatre, she reminded herself. Bentman took her elbow, guiding her into the dimming orchestra stalls.

Margaret knew the subject of the play. She knew it was supposed to be great art. However she did not know how personally it would affect her. The men were so rigid and the women so misunderstood. Scapegoats. You learned a lot about scapegoats in the Tenderloin. Ernie, Roberto, even Chrissie were scapegoats. Mr M tried to fire Chrissie when she was organizing the union. He called her a communist. Little did he know that Chrissie was more radical than any communist ever thought of being. Margaret shifted awkwardly in her seat, finally settling back to watch the play.

Now she became conscious of Bentman's manly presence next to her, the scent of his aftershave, the underlying, slightly tart odor of his sweat which she liked. Funny how you could enjoy the sweat of some people, a mustiness that didn't offend at all, unlike the sour perspiration of strangers on the bus. Even without looking at him, Margaret was aware of his size — the height from which his even breath fell, the length his leg stretched across the floor, the width of his shoulder which closed her off from the whispers and coughs of the audience behind. Reverend Parris in this play was a religious widower too, but so different from Roger, so harsh. He used his religion to scourge people. Roger was the opposite. Thoughtful, kind to the point of being self-effacing.

Lights rose for intermission. Bentman asked if she wanted to leave for a drink or a smoke. She declined both with equal alacrity. So they sat in their velvet chairs, watching the crowds walk up toward the doors, as if deserting a sinking ship. Margaret had never noticed how tilted theatres were. Truth was, she had never before sat in the stalls. It was exciting being this close to the stage and peering up at the grand chandeliers hanging from the distant ceiling.

'Perfect parallels with McCarthyism on the whole,' Bentman

was saying.

Margaret did not admit that she had liked Senator McCarthy at first, had admired his staunch patriotism. 'Actually, I keep forgetting about the 50s,' she said. 'The play seems much more current.'

Bentman told her how *The Crucible* was first received, about the charges of subversion, the obstacles in producing it, and the subsequent acknowledgement as a classic.

'How interesting,' Margaret managed. She told herself to pay closer attention, to respond intelligently, but she was too distracted. She was enthralled by the elegant walls and the fur coats and the realistic set which she could see more fully now that the lights were up. She must pay attention. Everything was interesting. That was the dilemma. She didn't know where to concentrate. Always her problem — focus; that's why she liked the excitement of the news stand with Pop better than she liked school. She could get lost in Bentman's voice. Clear and deep. Educated without being pretentious. Thoughtful, slow, with pauses. Pauses . . . he was pausing . . . perhaps he had asked her a question.

He gestured in the direction of Kevin Sinclair. 'So the father and son are feuding about the election now?'

'Yes,' tsked Margaret, relieved that she had a clear answer. 'I don't know what to do. I don't want to take sides.'

'Absolutely right,' Bentman concurred as the lights blinked and the passengers returned to the ship. 'That election has caused enough strife. Stay out of family feuds.' He sighed with a breath that moved his whole body. 'We used to vote by marking ballots; now apparently we do it with rocks and guns. Horrible, that firebombing of Marissa Washington's office. Still, the best approach is to stay out of the mess, to conduct your civic duty, of course, but to stay out of the mess.'

Margaret tried very hard to gag Chrissie who was nag-nag-nagging at the back of her head.

In fact Chrissie disappeared rather quickly. First, Margaret found herself straining to hear the troubled voice of John Proctor. Then she felt Roger Bentman's hand, moving from the velvet arm of the chair, reaching for her own hand, holding it warmly, securely, as if this were the most natural movement in the world.

Twelve

'So why don't you admit what's really bothering you?' Ernie refilled Chrissie's glass from the nearly empty pitcher of lager. He moved his chair closer and watched her with those piney green eyes which weren't any less lustrous in the smoky haze of the Edinburgh Castle. As Douglas said, this pub proved that you could find everything on Geary Street.

Chrissie snapped, 'I would have gone to Vienna if I wanted Sigmund Freud. I presumed you invited me here as a friend, not as a patient.'

Actually, she had been fully aware of his therapeutic intent all evening. She noticed how he had taken her to the little fish 'n chips place which must have curdled his vegetarian soul. How he had examined the framed travel brochure photos of Ayrshire and asked dutifully whether she remembered home like that. How he had insulted the woman behind the counter with his elastic good will by inquiring what part of Scotland she was from and, upon hearing 'Belfast', commenting that their accents were similar! It wasn't for himself that he had suggested drinking at the Edinburgh Castle with its jukebox reels and squads of hearty young men ogling thin young women. She knew how much he preferred those bars in the Castro where he could sit at a window table, keeping an eye on the procession inside and out. She knew that he was being kind and she at least owed him candor. But she wasn't ready.

'That Kevin!' Chrissie shook her head. 'The way he twists Margaret around his little finger!' She sipped foam from the top of her glass. A little too cold, but she had never found an American bar where the lager was warm enough. 'She's not a stupid woman.' Chrissie sounded as if she were trying to convince herself. 'Yet she's completely taken in by his little trinkets and infectious flowers. He's always had her heart, ever since he was a lad. Prime recipient for her perpetual mothering.'

Ernie enjoyed Chrissie's sarcasm, the edge from which she challenged the rest of humanity. However, he believed she was overdoing it about Kevin.

'I can't defend his politics,' Ernie mused. 'But he's relatively harmless. He's basically a misguided —'

'Little twit,' Chrissie finished. 'So how can you champion someone who supports Carson?'

'Hold on.' Ernie emptied the pitcher into her glass. 'I didn't say Kevin was my best friend.'

'Everybody's your best friend, Ernie. That's your problem.'

'Thank you, Dr MacInnes.'

'*Touché*,' she nodded apologetically.

'Had an interesting dinner with Marissa and Gus last night,' Chrissie offered.

'Oh, yeah?' Ernie relaxed at the change in tone. 'She was resilent after the firebombing, Jesus. And now those death threats? I mean, does she take them seriously?'

'No.' Chrissie closed her eyes momentarily. 'The initial panic has passed. She's a real veteran. It's only made her tougher.' Chrissie took a long drink. 'And the firebombing proved a bloody stupid tactic because it simply gained Marissa masses of sympathy.'

'I'd like to know her,' he said. 'Funny about politics, all of us working on campaigns, arguing about Marissa Washington and Jake Carson and we don't really know them personally. In some ways they're peripheral.'

'That's the way democracy used to be,' Chrissie declared. 'Aye, when we voted on issues instead of individual . . .'

'What's her apartment like?' Ernie asked.

Chrissie bristled and then appreciated Ernie's interruption. Crikey, she was grouchy tonight. 'Well, it's nothing to pique your interior decorating soul. Nice enough. After all, Gus is a lawyer and Marissa has some old savings from teaching. But simple, you know. And they stayed downtown, which is a lot more than most people who touch success.'

'You're proud of this friendship.' He refilled their glasses from a fresh pitcher.

Chrissie nodded. 'They're good people. I know that sounds Pollyanna. Still, they work hard and they're idealistic. We go back a long way, to civil rights and those tenants protests in the late 50s and then school nutrition programs. Marissa gave me my first bottle of lavender cologne. They're my oldest friends here, except for Douglas and Margaret.'

'Odd, the people in our neighborhood,' Ernie ruminated, 'Roberto, the raging Trot. Douglas, the sweet and sour cynic. Marissa, Gus, Gudrun, Margaret. Where else would you find us all working together?'

'Don't count on Margaret,' she said brusquely.

'Surely she's for Marissa. I mean she was at Glide. She knows about Carson's threats.'

'She's been spending quite a bit of time with the Reverend,' said Chrissie.

'And they talk politics?' asked Ernie, his attention diverted by the entrance of a delicate, fair-haired man who was obviously not seeking a Scottish lass. The man noticed Ernie, smiled demurely, and sauntered over to the bar. With exemplary willpower, Ernie returned to his friend.

Chrissie softened, conscious of Ernie's sacrifice. Then her eyes grew distant. 'As Margaret told me yesterday, 'We used to vote by marking ballots. Now we do it with rocks and guns. The best approach is to stay out of it, to conduct our civic duty, but to stay out of it.'

'Wonder where she got those lines,' grimaced Ernie.

'Exactly.' Chrissie sipped the lager which was now becoming tolerably warm.

'So how do you feel?'

'Bloody angry, how do you think I feel?' She told herself not to vent her jealously on Ernie. Why was she upset about this silly flirtation? Was it the absurdity of Bentman, himself? Or was she just fed up with Margaret's eternal search for the holy male?

'Bloody angry,' he imitated her accent. 'Seriously, though, it's harmless. I mean he's giving her a good time. She said he took her to the theatre last week. She deserves a little diversion.'

'Diversion? More like emotional kidnapping if you ask me.'

'Come on,' he coaxed. 'It's just a pleasant little friendship. It's not as if they're spring chickens hopping into bed with each other.'

'Who are you to make assumptions about who can and can't hop into bed with whom?' she exploded.

'Well . . . I . . . okay, you've got me. Ageist. At least.' he tried to make her laugh, 'Margaret doesn't have to worry about birth control.'

'Oh, shut up, will you,' Chrissie sighed. 'And take that ridiculous smirk off your face. Sometimes I wonder why I ever made friends with you, whether it was sheer desperation.'

It hurt. She had meant it to hurt. And acknowledging these two things, her pique dissolved.

'You're hard to keep up with.' He was subdued. 'Are you defending Margaret or criticizing her?'

'Truth is,' she looked sheepish, 'I just miss her a bit.'

'How do you mean,' he tried to flatten the therapeutic tone in his voice.

'She just isn't around as much — for Scrabble and movies and watching the news.'

He nodded, slowly rotating the pitcher between his heavily ringed hands.

'And when she is there, she isn't completely there.'

'Does she talk to you about him?'

'She wouldn't dare!' Chrissie swallowed the rest of her beer and raised her hand to the waiter for another pitcher.

'You really love her.'

'Of course I do. What are you getting at?'

His eyes lit on the gay man at the bar.

'Just keep your sexual preoccupations to yourself. Can't human beings love each other without labels?'

'I didn't say a thing.'

'I read minds.' Chrissie cleared her throat definitively.

'I've known that for years,' he said. 'I also know you love me.'

'Och, enough now, and pour me some beer before I pour it over you.'

On his way into the news shop, Roger Bentman was almost knocked down by a bearded young man who was leaving.

'Morning, Margaret.' He composed himself with exaggeration and watched through the glass door as the fellow strode down Geary Street. 'Lovely day,' he said.

'Yes.' she laughed at her own nervous excitement. During

86

the last weeks she had been caught between enjoying this romance and worrying how long it would last. Roger, on the other hand, seemed to be flourishing unequivocably.

'So the great debate is tomorrow night,' he observed.

Slocum growled at her feet. She had been very cool to the minister lately, as if she were jealous. It was like a plague. Slocum. Douglas. Chrissie. Why did they begrudge her a bit of happiness?

'Yes, after the evening news,' she said. 'Douglas is going to bring his television into the shop. Asking for trouble, I think.'

'The trouble has abated.' Roger frowned. 'There haven't been any "incidents", as the broadcasters say, since they announced this media event.'

'That's because Carson wants to take one good last aim *straight* at the title.' Douglas abruptly joined the discussion from behind.

Margaret imagined Douglas cast as the cantankerous ghost, appearing, as he always did, out of nowhere, out of your conscience. Quickly, she replayed the conversation with Roger relieved that nothing intimate had passed between them.

Kevin entered the shop, his arms filled with packages, and almost bumped into his father.

'Sorry,' he mumbled.

'You need a red flag with that wide load,' Douglas chided.

Hearing his father's voice, Kevin stopped and set down the parcels. He blanched, then tensed, then acquired a small grin. Margaret marvelled at the intricate hostility between father and son. This was like watching an ancestral duel.

'Sorry, Dad,' he said. And then gaining confidence, 'Just a few things for the business.'

'Porno magazines?' Douglas raised his voice.

'No,' Kevin answered instantly. 'Record books, file folders, desk pads and so on.'

'Yes,' Douglas persisted, turning to Margaret, 'did you know that my ambitious son has expanded his business?'

Margaret looked from Roger's drawn face to Kevin's downcast eyes to Douglas's angry frown. She resented being in the middle. She refused. Closing her eyes, she concentrated until she could hear Douglas's record — 'The Musical Offering', his favorite — then she pulled out her feather mop and attended to the cigarette racks.

'Yes, Mam,' Douglas continued. 'Opening more adult bookstores for our very neighborhood. Community.' he bowed to Roger. 'Just what the Tenderloin needs, a little "development". A few more enterprises where, for the price of a thin quarter, you can watch five-year-old girls being raped. And old women being bound and beaten. Yes, sir, nothing like a little free enterprise.' He exaggerated a W.C. Fields cadence. 'Another media shop. Like father, like son.' He surveyed the store with an outstretched hand.

Margaret hated Douglas at moments like this. Hated him for his hate. Illogical though it was, she felt that the porn shops were his fault. She stared at Douglas, as if to shame him, at least to quieten him. Roger was engrossed in an article on the front page of *The Los Angeles Times.*

Finally, Kevin spoke. 'It's not true. Sure, a couple of maga-zine stores leased the ground floor of our apartment building. I have no control over what they do. It's a free country.'

'Where did you learn that?' asked Douglas. 'Free for the taking?' Sure, when the takers have strong arms like Jake Carson. And my son. Ha, my son!' He turned and stalked back to his office.

Margaret tried to close her ears. She had never been able to escape their fights. *Why* did they struggle so?

Mute with fury, Kevin gathered his parcels. He managed to say to Margaret, 'I've got to go now. A lot of business. See you later.' As an afterthought, he turned to Roger and nodded courteously, 'Good day, Reverend.'

Once Kevin closed the door to the stairs, Roger leaned over the counter. 'A difficult situation, Margaret. For them. For you.'

'Yes,' she sighed gratefully. 'This real estate is the only job Kevin ever succeeded at. I can't tell if he's succeeding because Douglas hates it or vice versa.'

Bentman gave a resigned, but not unsympathetic, shrug.

She felt uncomfortable with the silence that followed. Almost tangible was the space between them.

'I wonder if I might make a bold request.' Roger moved closer.

Close enough for a kiss, Margaret wondered hazily. During

the last few weeks, despite Grandma's mottled mirror, she had felt prettier. No, just close enough, she understood, so that his words would be guarded from indiscreet listeners.

'Of course,' she said.

'Since I shan't really get to see you until Saturday — you'll be caught up in the debate here tomorrow night — I wonder if I might drop by your apartment for a few moments this evening.'

He followed a worry across her face.

'Not for long,' he said. 'After dinner — about eight — just to say hello.'

'I'd be delighted.'

Her only concern was how to get home in time to clean the studio before he arrived. Why couldn't she cultivate a little neatness? Oh, why was she so lazy? As for 'after dinner', apparently Roger had forgotten she worked until seven-thirty. So dinner would be one of those submarine sandwiches from Giorgio which she could eat while she vacuumed Slocum's fur from the couch. A pity that Roger wore dark suits which picked up every stubborn dog hair.

The dome clock chimed eight. The doorbell made it nine.

Ever punctual. Margaret imagined he had to be prompt after a life of giving services. You can't do Sunday without the minister. She liked the consideration he showed to her and others. Pausing before Grandma's mirror, she fluffed out the back of her hair. Time for another henna already, quite disappointing. She switched down one of the lamps. Good. A nice soft light. She had given up trying to hide her wrinkles — had even come to like the ones around her eyes. Still, she was proud of this dark hair. Chrissie urged her to 'go natural'. What was natural about grey when she had been coal black all her life?

He was carrying something. Not flowers, Margaret noted, a bottle.

'Cognac.' He spoke awkwardly. 'Given to me after a wedding last week. A man can't drink on his own, so I thought I'd share it with my favorite friend.' He kissed her cheek.

Slocum barked sharply. Getting no response from Margaret, she skulked into the kitchen and lay down heavily next to her bowl.

Graciously, Margaret accepted the bottle, cautioning herself to remember the night of the martini and to proceed slowly.

'I'm afraid I don't have,' she stumbled, 'anything to go with it.'

'You have glasses,' he grinned. 'And me.'

She offered him a seat and walked into the kitchen, unnerved that the evening was already going a little too fast for her.

His long, tapered fingers held the brandy glass as if it were a chalice. His baritone voice was certainly itself. She had a hard time believing their intimacy, believing she wasn't really still in the back pew daydreaming.

He was telling her how he had talked a man from jumping off the St Francis Hotel four years ago. How he had stayed with the man twelve hours. Yes, Margaret knew, she had read the story in *The Chronicle.* In fact, it was this incident which started her going to church again. She wasn't much interested in what religion could do for you in the next world. It seemed more important that she could enjoy this one first. And if Roger Bentman could talk somebody into life, she would try his church.

Slocum crept quietly into the room.

Relaxing back on the couch, Margaret moved her stockinged feet through Slocum's fur. She watched Roger's lips. She breathed in the sweet, fruity smell of the cognac and savored his voice.

Abruptly, he slid closer. 'You live so attentively.' He looked at her and then took a long sip.

'Pardon?' She was at once disappointed by the end to their meditative stillness and excited by his closeness. She reminded herself that he was a man of God, that her urges were premature.

'I often watch your face when I preach. You're always following. Sometimes you're ahead of me.'

'Ahead?' Margaret asked, putting down the brandy with distress. She had only taken a sip or two. She watched Slocum move back to the kitchen.

'An inspiration.' He took her hand.

She felt such fondness. She knew they would kiss next. Carefully, she took in the smile on his lips, the grey in his eyes. He set down the glass and drew her toward him. This was like their first kiss, after the theatre, and the others since. Gentle, sweet, sure. Yet now there was something else, something deeper and more urgent. She was conscious of his sweat, of the warmth of his breath, of the loosening in her own body. He held her more closely and she reached her arms around his back as if he were a lifeguard pulling her from the ocean. *Rye beach in July. Mom chasing Pop across miles of umbrellas, sand in her fist, ready to throw it, Pop laughing. She and Sylvia watching from their striped towel, understanding that for the moment they must stay with the picnic basket and the wallets, must play parents while Mom and Pop run through the sand.*

'Margaret,' he startled her. 'Margaret, I love you, I do.'

She drew back and searched his eyes.

'Ever since Florence passed on,' he whispered, 'I mean since I recovered from her death, I've been aware of you, your attentiveness at service, your cheerfulness in the shop, I . . .'

Margaret moved forward and kissed him again, partially from wanting him and partially from fear of hearing more. Man of God. Body of man.

They held each other for a long time, kissing, rocking, staring with shyness, astonishment and hunger.

'Dear one,' Roger murmured. He took her hand, leading her from the couch. He managed to pull down the Murphy bed with such dispatch that she later understood he must have been planning this movement for weeks.

Deftly he unbuttoned her yellow blouse. She remembered how sex felt as a girl of sixteen — fumbling, breathlessness, guilt, hurry — and she was glad to be seventy years old. Here was a man seasoned in eros, softly rolling his palm over the nylon slip until her nipples hardened, carefully removing the skirt, reaching up between her thighs to find her moistness and then pulling back, allowing her to unbutton his shirt, to kiss the sleek grey hairs on his chest, to move her hand beneath the waistband of his pants and to touch the hard tenderness that had risen for her. She wished it might end here. She had always liked the beginning best, the promise.

He continued to surprise her, tugging down the strap of her

91

slip with his teeth, touching her nipples first with his tongue. Biting gently, licking, biting, licking, biting, lickbitelickbite in a rhythm she thought might transport her to the ceiling. She was stretching in pleasure before she had a chance to be embarrassed by the folds of age gathered around her body. Gently again, he pulled the slip over her head and removed her pants. She reached down to touch him and found he had shed his clothes, like a lizard might slip from unserviceable skin. They lay side by side touching and stroking.

Circles. Round, wet circles on her belly. The belly of Janey and Rob and Michael. She often forgot it was her belly too. Round and round and round and round and down until he was inside her with his tongue, his wet hungry tongue reaching deep into her body, this thumb making music on her clitoris. Yes, this man was a caretaker. And bolder than she could have hoped. The blue spark of it all astonished her. Electric came the aftershocks: one, two, three, like the last earthquake. He kissed her full on the labia. She drew him on top. He entered her — oh, the satisfaction of this linking — and they rocked until they reached separate peaks.

Afterward (How much later? Impossible to tell from night outside the window. For the downtown night was always stolen by neons and auto horns. Had she slept? Had he slept?) sometime afterward, he turned to her and said, 'I love you Margaret.' She looked in his eyes and nodded, watching him fall off to sleep, wondering when she might have to answer.

Thirteen

Douglas had insisted on dragging his color TV to the front of the shop for the debate. Margaret warned him that it would impede business, that people would just stand about, getting in the way of customers.

'Nonsense,' he sniffed. 'Look at all the people who hover around store windows watching television. It might encourage trade. Besides,' he drew back his shoulders, 'do you think all I care about is selling a few newspapers? This could be a real service to the "community".'

Margaret could not tell if he were being sarcastic and she decided not to think about it.

By seven o'clock, the shop was crowded, Slocum barking to greet Mrs Dougal, Crazy Captain George, Ernie, Gudrun, Harvey Roberto, Mr Poulos, Chrissie.

Chrissie! Margaret started. She had agreed to go with Chrissie and the others for a drink at the Paddock. And last night, in the haze of last night, she had agreed to drop by the Clift with Roger for a nightcap. They would both be irritated with her. No, Chrissie would be fuming. She wondered, for the twentieth time today, whether the events of the previous evening had actually happened.

Then, as if she had summoned him, in walked Roger Bentman, a broad grin on his scrubbed face and a red rose in his hand. Noticing Chrissie, he lowered the flower to his side, but it was too late. Chrissie had smelled the rose as well as seen it.

Ernie, observing Chrissie's rebuff, greeted him warmly, 'The debate, Reverend, between Jake Carson and Marissa Washington. It's about to start. You're just in time.'

'Thanks,' said Roger. His eyes averted from Chrissie, he nodded formally to Margaret and Douglas Sinclair.

The television spoke stupidly into the shop. Chrissie imagined KPRO addressing the magazines and paperbacks and newspapers, as if they were all co-operating in some vast information machine.

'Tomorrow's weather,' clowned the meteorologist, moving his red pen over a satellite photograph which Margaret knew they were supposed to believe was the Pacific Coast, 'will be warm and sunny. Unless,' his smile exposed a row of giant white teeth which might have been borrowed from a Colgate commercial, 'unless it's cold and rainy.'

Margaret reached down and stroked Slocum's warm neck. She never believed in these meteorologists. For all their barometers and thermometers, they were never as accurate as her corns.

'Cold and rainy,' she heard someone say. Herself.

'What?' Douglas twisted the aerial to improve the focus.

'Her corns,' interpreted Chrissie. 'Margaret tells the weather by her corns.'

Mortified — more by herself or Chrissie? She didn't know. Margaret grinned to make the best of it. Inadvertently, she looked to Roger, who was laughing with the rest of them. Of course he knew about her corns. She could still feel his strong fingers massaging the soles of her feet. ('That's wonderful,' she had said. 'My job,' he had answered, 'guardian of souls.' They had giggled together.) Observing him now, Margaret heard the intimacy of last night in his laugh. So Chrissie's subterfuge had backfired.

'An educated woman,' Ernie commended. 'I've always said Margaret Sawyer is an educated woman right down to her toes.'

Margaret rolled her eyes at Ernie.

In the midst of this silliness, the door opened, admitting Kevin. He rendered a sweet smile to Margaret, then faced his father, 'Evening, Dad. I see you've opened a movie house. Where's the popcorn stand?'

Exposed by the general silence, Sinclair coughed sharply.

A resonant voice invaded; 'Tonight's regular programming has been pre-empted by a public service of KPRO. A debate for one of the most controversial seats on the San Francisco Board of Supervisors.'

Douglas tsked nervously. 'How can a seat be "controversial"? Where were these people educated?'

'Yeah, even an immigrant like me,' Roberto joined in,

'knows that a seat can't be controversial. "Hot" maybe, but not controversial.'

'Shhh,' Chrissie scowled. 'You two grammarians can adjourn to the back room.'

Leave it to Chrissie to tell Douglas what to do in his own shop, considered Margaret. Silence greeted Marissa's appearance on the screen. Her face was bright, a little shiny under the lights, proud, intelligent, edged with defiance. Carson, in his attempt at professionalism, looked slick, thought Margaret. If there were a power shortage, Marissa would win the debate right now. No, Margaret admonished herself, she knew how television could distort people's images. Why that time ten years ago when Janey had been interviewed an KPRO about being a draft resister – while the interviewer insisted that a woman couldn't be a draft resister – Janey didn't look at all like Janey. She looked like some ragamuffin in jeans and a t-shirt. And her nose – so long – Lord, that wasn't her nose. Tonight, Margaret would pay particular attention to the candidates' platforms, to Carson's platform. After all, Kevin must have good reasons for supporting him.

'The downtown is the heart of San Francisco.' Carson was speaking confidently, almost aggressively. 'It is from here that we must grow and build. Commercial investment could revitalize the Tenderloin and the entire city.'

Carson was a strong man, Margaret would give him that. And she did agree with his beliefs in a commercial downtown San Francisco. She could feel Chrissie wince in back of her and refused to look around. She glanced to her right where Roger's face was cool, observant. Perhaps he was the only person here who was actually listening to the candidates.

Marissa led off with what to Margaret's mind was an equally convincing speech about poverty and homelessness in the Tenderloin. Then she described the increase of violent crime. Frankly, Margaret didn't think it did much good to repeat such things on television, because it might give people ideas – the off-balance people you often saw on the streets. But then, they didn't watch political debates.

'I would like to know what Mr Carson thinks of all this violence.' Marissa faced him, instead of the camera, which Carson had addressed. 'What, for instance, do you think about the smashing of windows displaying my signs or about the destruction of my headquarters or about the breaking of my campaign manager's arm?'

'No one can pin that stuff on him,' Kevin blurted. 'There's no evidence,' he lowered his voice.

'We need a death before it stops?' demanded Roberto.

Margaret gave each man an icy glare. 'Shhh.'

'My esteemed opponent does me little honor,' said Carson, 'in not accepting my sincere concern about these incidents. I hope she recalls the letter I sent upon the senseless destruction of her office.'

Marissa looked straight at the camera. 'I'm not likely to forget either the incident or the letter.'

'That a girl,' cheered Chrissie. 'Give it to him.'

Harvey smiled appreciatively.

Kevin cleared his throat. Without saying goodnight, he walked up to his office.

Margaret stared at Chrissie, but her friend was glued to the screen, waiting for Carson to reply to Marissa's next challenge.

'See, he can't even answer the questions without a research assistant,' Douglas sneered.

Carson looked down at the podium, shuffling papers, waiting for his assistant to bring a portfolio. 'Just wanted to present all the background on my official position. This is something worked out after months of research and care.'

'Such care that you can't remember the first word,' chided Ernie.

'*Ja*,' Gudrun agreed, moving closer to Ernie.

He inched away, embarrassed but worried about hurting her feelings. 'Really, he could have practiced for this.'

Shhh,' Margaret glared again.

'God damn it, Margaret, this isn't a library,' said Douglas. Margaret was taken aback by his tone and surprised by his defense of Ernie. Perhaps she *was* being a little officious, but how was a person to follow?

Then Margaret felt a chill tickle down her neck. Who was the man delivering Carson's notebook? A boy, really, his hair an artificial brass, thanks to Douglas's broken color monitor. He looked so familiar. Now, how would she know one of Carson's aides? Ridiculous. Still, she glanced around to see if anyone else noticed him. Ernie was whispering to Roberto. Gudrun was watching Ernie. Chrissie and Douglas shared some private joke. Captain George, Mrs Dougal and Mr Poulos regarded the screen impassively.

As the young man walked off camera, Carson beamed. 'I'd like to quote a survey we conducted of twelve cities.'

Rubbing her feet along Slocum's back, Margaret longed to bury her aching corns in the warm fur.

'Damn him,' Douglas shouted. 'Sure he'd quote Seattle. What the hell has Seattle got to do with us? It's a totally different situation.'

'Perhaps you should be debating the gentleman,' Mr Poulos interposed, then retreated, obviously thinking better of reprimanding Douglas Sinclair.

'They're just making promises and promises,' said Captain George in his wee, high voice as he twiddled a lock of his silvery hair. Chrissie wondered, was it an attempt to mediate between Douglas and Poulos or just one of his usual prophesies about the hopelessness of contemporary reality?

Finally the debate was over. Margaret felt as if it had taken two hours rather than one. However, when KPRO returned to regularly scheduled programming, the re-runs of 'Leave It To Beaver' were on time.

Roberto stomped his foot. 'She's won already. I say we drink to celebrate. How about adjourning to the Paddock for *unos tragos*!'

'Capital,' said Ernie, moving too slowly from Gudrun, who linked his arm and began singing as if she'd already made a few toasts, 'Home, Home on the Range'.

Chrissie and Douglas were chuckling again. Margaret looked to Roger, who seemed uncomfortable. And Chrissie, noticing their exchange, called, 'Come on, Father, this is one part of the downtown community you should know.'

'Thank you.' Roger would not rise to her bait. 'I'd love to. But another time. I've got to prepare a noon lecture. And I've been fighting a cold.'

'Another time,' Chrissie nodded happily. Then she looked expectantly at Margaret.

'Yes, I'll come along,' she said. Although she was exhausted, she knew she couldn't sleep for hours. 'I just have to explain the day's receipts to Luis. You all go on. Slocum and I will catch up.'

As the others were leaving, Roger turned to Margaret, 'So I'll see you on Saturday? We still have our date for Sausalito?'

Had Chrissie heard? She didn't turn around, but Margaret noticed her friend's spine stiffen. Why should she feel so badly? They had made no plans for Saturday. She had a perfect right to go out with Roger. Sometimes Margaret felt as if she were having two affairs. She believed she could love both Chrissie and Roger well. She felt no conflict in her affections. However, deep down, she felt guilty, afraid that she didn't deserve them. Afraid, so afraid. Wild fears. Afraid that when each person learned how much she meant to the other, they would both leave. Afraid she would go mad juggling schedules and feelings. Even afraid that they might take off together — now that was a laugh — the Reverend and Chrissie.

'Margaret,' he roused her, 'we still have our plan for Saturday?' He picked the tired rose from a low shelf where he had put it until they were alone.

She stared at the rose and listened to his voice as Chrissie might. A little too eager. Even pleading. She had a terrible doubt. How strong would this man be without his God, a man alone, as she had been a woman alone for years. She found the thought irreverent, blasphemous. She put it out of her mind and registered his serious grey eyes.

'Of course, Roger,' she smiled. 'I'm looking forward to it.'

By the time she got to the Paddock Lounge, they were all well into their second round.

'Sit by me, Mama,' said Roberto, pointing to the chair between himself and Chrissie. 'Come have some peanuts and pretzels.'

Ruefully she regarded the contents of the bowls. Perhaps this is what she should have served Roger that evening. Perhaps potato chips were out of style. She and the kids used to eat them on Friday nights, but perhaps they were for kids, that particular kind of junk food. Peanuts were sophisticated. More modern. Protein at least.

'Well, you're somber,' said Douglas.

'No, just sober,' declared Ernie, offering his Manhattan.

Gratefully, she sipped, her eyes averted from Chrissie, who had not bothered to greet her.

Soon they were caught up, praising Marissa's passionate delivery and proclaiming the evening's success.

'She won the election tonight,' declared Harvey.

'Of course we have another person to thank for that,' said Roberto.

'Jake Carson,' he snickered. 'Ave Maria, calling for a development file in the middle of the debate!' They laughed with him.

Eventually Margaret slipped into good cheer. She laughed and relaxed and even spoke to Chrissie. Her friend seemed to loosen, too, with questions about Janey's letter and the photos Rob had sent from Fairbanks.

Chrissie couldn't help it. The more Margaret relaxed, the angrier she grew. She had known the woman for years, had seen her through thick and . . . well, through lots of thicks. Now Margaret was hiding the truth about Roger. It could be serious. Margaret was soppy enough to move into the fellow's manse — or whatever the American equivalent was called — and live out her life in blessed mediocrity. Sad how she could drop their friendship for a man. Sad, no, Chrissie felt frightened. Harshly, she rubbed against the arthritic pain stealing through her left hand. So much for their trip to Hawaii, she sighed, so much for their friendship. This week, Margaret had hardly had time for her, being too 'busy' or 'tired', one resulting from the other no doubt.

'So how about Saturday?' Chrissie asked in spite of herself.

'Pardon?' Margaret was startled by the change in tone and unsure of what Chrissie had overheard in the shop. Was she calling her hand about Roger or was she simply inviting her to go shopping? She decided not to be defensive.

'I'm busy Saturday,' said Margaret. 'Could we do something next week? Go to the tea house or perhaps to . . .'

'Busy,' repeated Chrissie. She knew that the third Scotch had made her too stubborn.

'I'm going to Sausalito,' Margaret said evenly, 'with Roger.'

' "Roger", is it?' asked Chrissie. 'It was "Reverend Bentman" last week. Lost your respect for the cloth?'

Margaret did feel uncomfortable using his first name in public. At church, certainly, she could still say 'Reverend'.

However, at the news shop, she felt awkward. She hadn't used a name at all. She said 'Roger' to herself. Thus it was 'Roger' that slipped out to Chrissie.

When her friend didn't answer, Chrissie insisted, 'Well just what have you and "Roger" been doing?' Immediately, she regretted this. Drink always made her mind race, as if it had been released from a steam roller. Damn alcohol had the opposite effect on Margaret, calming her slower than ever.

'We've been having a good time.' Margaret spoke more coyly than she felt. Chrissie made her belligerent. She glanced at their companions, glad to find them still debating about the debate. 'Besides,' she whispered, 'this isn't the place to discuss it.'

'Truce.' Chrissie lifted her glass and clinked Margaret's, grateful her friend had provided a way out. 'For tonight.'

'Truce?' inquired Ernie, leaning away from Gudrun. 'If you've got Chrissie to agree to peacemaking, I'm impressed. Truce on what?'

'Never mind,' answered Margaret.

Chrissie thought, the question is — for how long?

In bed later that night, Margaret wondered what Chrissie knew. Could she tell they had slept together? Margaret grinned to herself in the dim room, land of the midnight neon, Rob called it. She thought back to school when her best friend Loretta Ribman could tell she had been necking with Richard Lodart in the park. Come to think of it, Chrissie resembled Loretta Ribman in a number of ways.

Fourteen

'Hawaii,' declared Douglas, raising his Mummer's coffee mug. 'Here's to Alohaland.' He turned his head to cough, stifling the depth of it, because he couldn't bear Chrissie's interrogation about doctors and X-rays. 'Why are you taking her there?'

Irritated, Chrissie studied her watch. The black and white Timex, a gift from Ernie on her last birthday, had a minute hand, hour hand and real numbers. She hated those damn digital watches, especially the ones that had to be lit by the wearer. Anti-social was what they were. Chrissie saw that she had eight minutes left of her break. Why did she waste her precious free time on Douglas? She was as bothered by his refusal to take care of himself as by his patronizing attitude toward Margaret.

'I'm not *taking* her anywhere,' said Chrissie. 'We're going together. For a holiday.'

'To learn the hula? When you come back we could rent out the Alcazar.'

'To rest our old bones,' contradicted Chrissie. Absently she glanced over to her station to make sure Jeannette was able to cope with all the tables. 'To take a holiday from elections and weary work schedules and oppressive bosses.'

'That last line is worthy of Roberto.' Douglas cleared his throat. 'Bosses. Speak for Mr M if you like, but ask Margaret if I'm her oppressor.'

'Margaret doesn't understand the word,' said Chrissie. 'I keep telling you that split shift is terrible for her health.'

'What did you say about not taking care of Margaret?' Douglas was exasperated, yet delighted at catching Chrissie out. 'Besides, she *likes* that shift. Says it keeps her busy. Keeps her from being lonely.'

'That won't be a problem now — with the messiah.'

Douglas coughed, holding back nothing now, spitting enough phlegm to saturate the pink and white Mummer's napkin.

Chrissie studied the color of the phlegm with the unself-conscious scrutiny that comes after long friendship. They had always had a low grade competition for Margaret's attention. Douglas was too hurt by what had happened to Louise and then to Kevin to acknowledge his affection as more than a joke. The competition made no sense, Chrissie understood, because Margaret loved them each differently. Now that Bentman had raised his ugly heart, she and Douglas were unconditional allies.

'God's gift to the "downtown community",' snarled Douglas. '*What* can she see in him?'

'Probably the same thing we see in her. Goodness.'

'Ridiculous comparison.' Douglas reddened. 'Margaret is a simple, honest, kind woman. He's a simpering weakling.'

'He attempts to practice virtue,' said Chrissie, herself a little hoarse. Was she catching Douglas's cold? 'Instead of merely being attracted to it.'

Douglas coughed again, as if asserting that virtue were nothing to which he aspired.

Chrissie considered how much Margaret resembled Louise Sinclair. So feminine. Sweet. Delicate. Poor Louise had never been quite well after Kevin's birth. Such a tragedy when she died two years later with her stillborn girl. Chrissie used to speculate what would have happened to Douglas if Louise had lived. Surely he wouldn't have become an old man at forty. And Kevin? She didn't believe any of that hooha about children needing their mothers' complete attention. Still, Kevin needed something. Douglas had gone into a horrible depression after her death. He hardly noticed Kevin until . . . until it was too late. Chrissie knew she should have more sympathy with the chap. But she wished he hadn't always been so damn stupid.

'Virtue.' Douglas sucked the black coffee. 'Apparently my son isn't even attracted to it.'

Chrissie was taken aback. This was the first time in months that Douglas had calmly contemplated his son. Often he seemed to pretend Kevin didn't exist. When Kevin was young, Douglas was so busy selling papers, trying to save enough money for the shop, that he didn't have much time. Maybe that was another reason for . . . och, who could comprehend behavior? Still, she did want to understand Kevin, to gain some wit against the destructiveness. Carson had gained several percentage points last week. If they weren't careful, he would win the election.

'Porn shops. You know his latest enterprise is peep shows and adult movies. Not directly, oh, no. My tasteful son observes a pretense of honor. He's just rented four storefronts to those goons.'

Chrissie shook her head, remembering that one of those shops previously had been a drop-in center for drug-dependent men, Marissa's oldest project.

'Money. That's all he cares about. What kind of example did I set? Is this because we were always so tight for cash?'

Chrissie raised one eyebrow. 'Now that is gall, taking responsibility for someone else's life.'

'I must have had some effect on him, damn it, Chrissie. I raised him alone for twenty years.'

'Alone?'

'You helped, okay, and Margaret, when he was sick or on vacation from school. However I bear the burden for his standards.'

'You bear a lot of burdens.'

'Well, look at Roberto,' he said. 'Hardworking. Good to his daughters. Honest. Why couldn't *he* have been my son.'

'He is, in a way,' she sighed. 'Besides, you would go batty from his politics in ten minutes. If he were your son you wouldn't get along with him at all.'

Chrissie wasn't sure if she were defending Kevin or soothing Douglas or arguing just because this family guilt was absurd. She looked away for a moment as a ragged woman stole in the door and headed straight for an uncleared table. The woman moved as if programmed, cleaning off extra bread, scraps of bacon, pats of butter. She was just about to reach the next table when Jeannette gently directed her out the door. One of the worst parts of the job, Chrissie reckoned, was bouncing these people. But you didn't want to get a reputation as an easy mark. Some of them stole tips. Just last week she had lost two dollars that way.

'I don't get it,' Douglas said. 'If he hates me so much why doesn't he move? Why does he insist on that damn office?'

103

'Why don't you kick him out?'

'I keep hoping,' said Douglas. 'For what, I don't know.'

'Hope,' gasped Chrissie. 'Dour Douglas Sinclair accused of hope. No jury could bring a conviction.'

'Jury?' came a mock hysterical query from across the floor. She turned to find Ernie skirting a table, gracefully balancing a piece of pie, a pot of tea and a mug. Gudrun must have cut the pie. It was twice normal size. That woman was unswerving in her seduction, right enough.

'Conviction?' asked Ernie. 'They've finally arrested Jake Carson?'

Douglas moved over in the booth, still rather wary of Ernie. Chrissie watched the two men settle, like jays on an unsteady branch. Ernie dug into his food with gusto. Douglas watched. Chrissie recalled Douglas's early complaints about Ernie — that he was narcissistic and that he might try to harass Kevin. Trust had grown during recent years. And once, Douglas confided to Chrissie that Ernie had too much pride to choose Kevin. Anyway, since the beginning of Marissa's compaign, Ernie and Douglas had clearly become friends.

'No, I think he's purchased the police department,' Chrissie answered.

'I'll speak to Charles about that.' Ernie winked confidentially to Chrissie.

'Charles Hunter? What do you know about Hunter?' demanded Douglas. He's a law and order cowboy if you ask me. Too friendly with my upright son. What do you know about him?'

Embarrassed, Ernie shrugged and looked at Chrissie. Chrissie looked at her watch.

'How are Marissa's spirits?' Ernie asked.

'Could be better,' said Chrissie. 'We had a drink last night and she doesn't know where the next penny's coming from. It cost a lot to regroup after the fire. And Carson has invested more than we imagined. The parties. The press coverage. The 'personal attentions' to property owners. The phoney social conscience efforts — like that free turkey dinner at St Anthony's next week. Marissa just doesn't have that kind of bank account.'

'Money, volunteers, influence.' Ernie forked the last of the pie. 'You got it, Marissa could use it.'

'Well, I'm allergic to meetings,' Douglas pulled out his checkbook, 'but . . .'

'All contributions welcome.' Chrissie felt a twinge, since it was the third check from Douglas this month. Tucking the donation into her apron, she yawned, stretched and stood. 'Back to Sunrise Omelettes and other surprises.'

'Don't break your back running around for Mr M.' Douglas's voice approached concern.

'I just keep thinking about Hawaii,' said Chrissie, 'counting the tips for Alohaland.'

Fifteen

Their ride across the Golden Gate Bridge was beautiful, Margaret was sure it was beautiful. She sat back in Roger's car, trying to enjoy the blue sky and the golden Marin hills. Wonderful how the Pacific below turned from turquoise to teal to robin's egg blue depending on the time of day and the angle of the sun. She knew because Sausalito was one of Chrissie's favorite expeditions. They would take the bus, poke around the shops and eat in a little fish 'n chips place. The trip to Sausalito was beautiful, Margaret reminded herself. She did notice that she couldn't see as much from Roger's window as she could see from the bus.

He was listening to classical music on KKHI and spoke to her only during the commercials for Taylor Wineries. She felt complimented by this, by the notion that they knew each other well enough for companionable silence. Today the quiet was disconcerting because it left so much room to worry about Chrissie. And Slocum. The dog had been sulking lately, especially when Roger was around. Of course Slocum would recover in time and so would Chrissie.

'First we'll go to the Trident,' he said. 'Then I'd like to show you the harbor. There's a splendid marina.'

'Lovely,' said Margaret. She had never found the right synonym, but now she was less self-conscious about her speech.

The Trident was crowded with flashy young people sipping pastel cocktails. Roger had had the foresight to make a reservation. 'Mr Bentman,' they called him, Margaret noticed, not 'Reverend'. Was this his choice or theirs?

The bay was choppy this afternoon, rather like her stomach. Windclear sky. Her mind wasn't clear; it was empty. She accepted the water glass from their waiter with urgent gratitude. Something to occupy her mouth. The calamari, she observed, was three times the price of the fish 'n chips she and Chrissie usually ordered. Still, she acquiesced to

Roger's recommendation. He was having oysters. And they would share.

Margaret relished his affection. In a moment of sweetness last night, he told her that he had been waiting for her. He and Florence had not made love during the last ten years. Frustrating, but they had become good friends. Since he met many lonely women in his work, he had had opportunities for infidelity. However, he was saving himself. During the two years since Florence's death, he realized that he had been saving himself for Margaret.

She looked across the table and returned his smile with a calm which she hoped would coat her stomach. The bread arrived not a moment too soon. She dug into the butter, dismissing all of Chrissie's admonitions about polyunsaturates. Why was Chrissie haunting her so? Did she use Chrissie to voice her own doubts? It was perfectly reasonable to visit Sausalito with Roger. She had a life of her own. She had a right to . . .

'. . . that he told me about?' Roger was asking.

'Pardon?' Margaret was angry at herself; she must seem a deaf old post.

'The robbery that Sinclair mentioned. Just last month. Did you have to testify?'

'They called me in.' Margaret was surprised at her evenness. 'It's one of the hazards of our,' she couldn't say 'community', 'of our neighborhood.'

He sighed and buttered a slice of bread.

'Really, it was very simple. The man came up to the counter and handed me a note. It said, "Give me your bills. the twenties first, then the tens," and so on. I attended the police line-up, but I couldn't decide. I know it's awful to say, but they all looked alike to me. And there was so much at stake, a man's future.'

Roger shook his head sympathetically. His wide, slate grey eyes were troubled, as if he were back in the shop watching the robber and the gun.

His response was so different from Chrissie's. 'Racist,' she had charged. 'What do you mean you couldn't tell them apart?' Of course Chrissie wouldn't be shocked at the robbery since she had gone through the ordeal half-a-dozen times herself.

She probably would have looked closer than Margaret, would have noticed the face. Yes, Margaret could see Chrissie's point. Still, how could she call her a racist for not wanting to make a mistake with someone's life?

'You still seem shaken over it,' said Roger.

'I guess I am.' Margaret sipped her white wine, thankful that Roger had had the presence of mind to order it. Much less lethal than martinis. 'Maybe that's what's bothering my stomach today.'

'Are you unwell?' His voice was deep, reassuring. 'The bread will be good for you, dear. Have another piece.'

Margaret usually grew nervous under attention. She never had much to say. So she kept a list of topics in her head for awkward moments. Movies. Music. Books. The weather.

Roger was watching two sailboats bob toward the marina. Following them with experienced concentration, his neck and shoulders tensed.

'Do you sail?' She was delighted with the extra topic.

'Yes,' he brightened. 'Or at least I once did. My brothers and I used to compete at the Yacht Club. We were very good. Planned to sail around the world. Then the world erupted in war. And it took one of my brothers.' He looked from the bay to Margaret's sad face. 'Yes, you know about that sort of thing.'

Margaret asked, wondering why she had never asked before, 'How did you get assigned to Brotherhood Church? It's so different from your life, your past, I mean.'

Roger sighed, 'You're wiser than I.'

She looked troubled.

'Oh, not that I regret the choice. It was *my* choice. At the time — twenty years ago — I was delighted that a parish was available in the city. I was ready to move back from Portland. I didn't realize that the Portland church was a lot closer to the San Francisco that I knew than the Tenderloin parish. Still, it's been good for me. I've learned a lot.'

Margaret tried to keep the conversation going between them, but she continued to imagine Chrissie and Douglas clearing their throats at his humility. So what if he were a little naïve politically? He truly cared for people. He was always on the alert to make you comfortable, unlike Chrissie,

for all her claims to social conscience. She regarded h
handsome fingers and recalled their first handshake
years before.

Then, as if on some radio wave, Roger added, 'D
remember when we met, Margaret? I do. I remembe
saying, "Welcome to the neighborhood," with worried
as if you were greeting a displaced Martian.'

She laughed.

'Margaret, you were the only one who was welc(
from the start, the only one who didn't dismiss me as
kind of Victorian missionary. And I can't say I blam
others — not with the attitudes I brought. The clothes I ,
If it hadn't been for Florence's support I don't know h
would have continued. You probably have no idea how
friendship mattered, how important it was to get that :
once a day from someone who *belonged* there.'

Margaret had never thought of herself as belonging t
She had always considered the neighborhood as a waysta
Often she daydreamed of moving to Walnut Creek, whe
was warmer, or to Chestnut Street, where she'd have a
of the water. She and Chrissie had been talking for ,
about pooling their pensions and buying a cottage.

As accustomed as he was to her sudden silences, h(
natural changing the topic. 'I guess Chrissie was the sam
you. A welcoming voice. Your friendship is very sp
isn't it?'

'Oh, yes,' she said. 'Chrissie and I are . . . planning
to Hawaii after the election.' To speak further about
retirement plans would be to disappoint Roger. To spe
further would be to betray Chrissie. That was the t
with this new 'relationship', as Ernie would call it. Th
affection she felt for Roger, the more guilt she felt
Chrissie.

'How nice,' he said coolly.

'Of course, if Marissa Washington loses the election
Chrissie will be too depressed to go.'

'She'll need a vacation all the more,' Roger suggest
what's the latest news? You're at the nerve center,
papers and direct reports from Chrissie and Kevin.'

'Well, it doesn't look good for her.' Margaret n(

wn sympathy for Marissa. 'Jake Carson got some very good publicity last week.'

'The Bosworth Club?'

Margaret nodded. 'And it seems Marissa's workers just can't bring in enough money.'

'Poor woman,' said Roger. 'She's a good person. I've talked with her. Well, this must make Kevin happy.'

'Yes,' Margaret said. 'He's been on top of the world this week. All the more guaranteed to sour his father. Oh, I wish those two would make peace.'

'Sad business,' said Roger, waving thanks to the waiter who had set huge lunches before them. Margaret wondered if she could ask for a doggie bag for herself, not for Slocum. This made her even more conscious of how she had neglected the dog recently. She sipped the wine, deciding that the restaurant was too sophisticated for doggie bags.

'Those two haven't stopped fighting since Kevin was a baby,' she said.

'Kevin doesn't get along with too many people as I understand.'

'He's really quite a sweet boy,' she said. 'He must feel some tie to his father; he could have left the upstairs office years ago.'

'So what's wrong with Douglas?'

'Douglas has his pressures. He's a worker, that one. He's made all he owns. Maybe there was never enough time for Kevin. And, quite frankly, I think he was rather disappointed that Kevin wasn't brilliant. He wanted his son to be a professor or a doctor or someone intellectual.'

'Margaret, you're very understanding.'

'Chrissie says "wishy-washy".' Why was Chrissie still bothering her? Perhaps she should just come out with the strain she felt between him and Chrissie.

Roger spoke first. 'What does she think of our involvement?'

She flinched at the word 'involvement'. Vocabulary was a clear distinction between him and Chrissie, between him and herself, for that matter. Margaret didn't have a better word. Now that was her distinction from Chrissie — Chrissie contracted, while she just flinched. She gazed out the window at a windsurfer dipping and flying through the waves.

He interpreted her silence. 'You haven't told her.'

'Only that we were going to Sausalito.' Margaret turned from the window to face him directly. 'Oh, that does sound pathetic, doesn't it?'

'I worry that Chrissie doesn't have much respect for me.'

Margaret was taken aback. She knew he was an honorable man, but she didn't know he could be so candid.

'She just has a different sense of what's good for the neighborhood.'

'And for you?' He noticed that she had hardly touched the calamari. 'Don't worry,' he put his hand on hers. 'I have no intention of stealing you away from Chrissie. You can have her friendship and me too.'

'She's just a strong-minded woman.' Margaret smiled. 'And perhaps a little possessive.' She felt her stomach relax.

'You've been a good friend to her,' said Roger. 'It will continue to be so. Now look at your lunch. You can take what's left in a doggie bag. However, do eat a bit more or I shall feel like a regular glutton.'

She relished his kindness. And his handsome ways. He wasn't dashing, yet he was sweet and genteel, rather like William Holden.

'And after a brisk walk around the marina, I was hoping to stop at the No Name Bar for Irish Coffee.'

She smiled again, thinking that it was very nice to be treated like a lady.

Sixteen

As Margaret peered through the wind for the Purple Peacock, she tried to figure out why Chrissie wanted to meet on Castro Street. Just to get out of the neighborhood for a bit, Chrissie had said. It must be more than that. Her voice had been high and tight. Margaret knew better than to ask questions. Purple Peacock. Silly name. Cold, crisp October weather, like the days before the first snowfall in New York. She'd been back in New York all afternoon. A memory tripped in the morning and she was back at Pop's news stand or the Jersey shore or the old apartment on Amsterdam.

'Excuse me,' came a voice next to her. Below her. Margaret looked over to see a baby carriage pushed by a man in a wheelchair. Michael. Two visions of Michael. So sweet in his carriage, the easiest of babies. Why couldn't he have come home, at least part of him? Disabled people could do almost anything nowadays. Michael in his carriage looked up at her as if there weren't anything but hope in the world. How had she failed him, them? Them, because she had also lost Janey to that war she still did not understand.

'Certainly,' said Margaret to the man in the wheelchair. She stepped aside so he could manoeuvre all eight wheels down the sidewalk ramp and into the street.

The street; the parade. She knew that Ernie hung out there on his 'social nights'. He had once taken her to a bar where men sat in windows watching other men walk by. He told her women were safe in this neighborhood and she didn't doubt it. Ernie called the inhabitants 'Castro Street Clones'. She noticed they did look similar, like Ernie in his short hair and flannel shirt and heavy boots. Wholesome, nice boys, actually. Such a contrast to the menacing mannequins in these windows. She stared at the rhinestone-studded leather pants with holes in the seat. The next store displayed gold-embossed whips and a silver tea set with a penis spout. Shocked, she moved to

112

the adjacent window: New Wave angora t-shirts; spats with photographs of Cary Grant under the heels. She thought about men wandering into conformity, into anonymity, into the playfulness of their childhoods.

The Purple Peacock flashed a multi-colored tail into the bright afternoon. Chrissie was waiting at the corner table, a stern contrast to the mellow boys around her, writing something in a notepad. Margaret wondered if she had ever seen Chrissie sitting absolutely still. Her friend looked up and waved.

'Why so late?' Chrissie took Margaret's coat roughly, as if her intention were to sell it on the black market rather than to make Margaret comfortable. 'Where did you come from, Siberia?'

Margaret read her watch. She was only ten minutes late. Chrissie's watch said fifteen minutes late, but she habitually set it five minutes fast.

'Sorry, I've been in such a tizzy.' Chrissie tried to calm down. After all, Margaret had agreed to traipse all the way over here so they could meet on neutral territory. Here she was, starting a fight already. 'Have some of my tea, hen.' She raised her hand to the waiter. 'We'll order another. You look like you're about to turn blue. Where did you get off the streetcar?'

'Not far from here.' Margaret closed her eyes and enjoyed the warm liquid draining down her throat. 'I got lost — Amsterdam Avenue, Michael, Janey, all of Ernie's stories. And the windows!'

'Margaret Sawyer,' Chrissie exclaimed fondly, 'only you could make a twenty block journey sound like a trip to Europe.'

Now that she felt warmer, Margaret began to take in the punk decor. Chrissie's tone annoyed her.

'Listen, there's nothing wrong with,' she watched Chrissie's jaw stiffen, 'me. But something's wrong with you, honey. What is it?'

Chrissie waited while their tea was served. Slowly she shredded the paper label attached to the used tea bag.

Was it about herself? Margaret's mind raced. About herself and Roger? She had already decided to tell Chrissie the whole truth.

'The campaign,' Chrissie began. What *did* she want from

Margaret? What difference could one person make? Still, she desperately needed Margaret to take a side, her side. She needed a sign of loyalty; this had become a test of their friendship.

Margaret waited.

'The campaign is getting more serious.' Chrissie poured the tea into her cup and, finding it too weak, poured it back into the aluminium pot.

Margaret unwrapped a cube of sugar and ate it.

'There have been more threats against Marissa.' Chrissie spoke rapidly, breathlessly, as if she were running. 'One attempt. They found part of an explosive device in her car. Margaret, I think Carson's people are mentally ill.'

'What can be done?' asked Margaret. 'Did you call the police?' She added, in spite of herself, 'All this over an election. Someone's life.'

'That's what the whole thing . . .' Chrissie's voice pierced the whining music. Several heads turned.

Margaret noticed that the men looked quite individual when they faced you.

Chrissie lowered her voice. 'That's what the whole thing is about. People's lives. Whether people still can *live* in the Tenderloin or whether they're going to turn our homes into grand hotels and massage parlors. Margaret, have you been awake during the last two months?'

Margaret drew a cold fury. 'Awake! Of course I've been awake. How could I sleep with rocks smashing against windows. Father and son yelling through both sides of my head. You railing and reeling from overwork and fear. Awake? I haven't been able to sleep more than four hours a night since this crazy business started.'

Chrissie held firm. 'Then why don't you do something? It's your neighborhood too. Why don't you come out canvassing?'

'I've told you a hundred times.' Margaret decreased her volume. 'I don't believe politics answers problems. It causes problems.'

'I suppose that's what you said to Janey and Michael?'

Chrissie regretted the sentence before she finished it. Yet she was livid. 'Margaret, you live in a dream world. You think people are curious, interesting, touching. I don't know what.

114

You meet me for coffee on Castro and you act like a tourist from Aberdeen. You think we live in a "community" rather than a slum. You imagine that if we all dropped by Douglas's shop and chatted, we could work out our differences. That Jake Carson and Marissa would develop a coalition. That Kevin and I would start attending the cinema together.'

Margaret's voice was soft and deliberate, 'I'm not a fool.'

'No, but you think . . .'

'I don't think difficulties are settled according to social theories or even according to votes. Certainly not according to violence. The trouble with this world is that people don't communicate. They don't try to understand each other.'

'Thank you, Madame Bentman.' Chrissie hated how he had got mixed up in all this.

'You *are* cruel.'

'You expect congratulations?' The anger drained from Chrissie's face. She was bewildered, exhausted. 'Is he what you really want, Margaret?'

Margaret rubbed her hand over Chrissie's cold knuckles. 'I don't know. I don't know what I have.' She couldn't discuss Roger now, not with all this anger between them. 'I do know I want your friendship. Don't tell me that's going to be another casualty of this election.'

'Then take the election seriously.' One thing at a time, Chrissie thought; she would avoid Margaret's love life for the moment. 'Look, I know I can get carried away about the campaign. That's why I wanted to meet here today, for a change of scene. I feel like we've been on the front lines for weeks. And we *have* to keep fighting. We need all the workers we can get. Won't you do something? Lick envelopes, something?'

Margaret reckoned that compromise was the only way to reach back to Chrissie. 'OK, I'll lick your envelopes, but that's it.'

'Great,' Chrissie's face was still taut. 'Friday night. There's a final fundraising drive. We're meeting at —' She halted at the expression on Margaret's face.

'I can't on Friday,' Margaret said.

'Bentman.' Chrissie closed her eyes.

Seventeen

'Monday morning,' Ernie exclaimed to no one in particular, to the crowds passing outside Douglas's shop. 'People are always tense on Monday morning.'

'It's the earthquake.' Charles Hunter leaned on Margaret's counter, sipping his coffee. 'Every time it happens, people ask themselves, "Is this the big one?"'

'What can you do?' shrugged Ernie. 'Frankly, I'd rather not think about it.'

'That's ridiculous,' said Chrissie. 'It's like nuclear war and cancer. People are so frightened that they run away, but hiding increases the danger.'

'The force has an earthquake alert,' said Charles. 'We had special training.'

'Did you always want to be a policeman?' Ernie's attention fluttered between Charles and the window.

Charles answered, 'Yes, I suppose, since I was ten or twelve.'

Chrissie watched, recalling Ernie's meaningful glance at Mummer's. The two men had been spending a lot of time chatting at the shop. She hadn't noticed them 'stepping out', as Ernie would say. However, Charles would have to be discreet. Police attitudes were less tolerant than official police policies. Romance, she considered. Romance everywhere under the shadow.

Chrissie turned to her old friend. 'So did you and Roger enjoy the film on Friday?'

'Yes,' Margaret said impassively. She pulled out the duster, attending to the cigarette case and the chewing gum rack.

'Slocum isn't missing you these days, I mean these nights?'

Ernie frowned a sharp warning. Chrissie adopted a more amiable tone, 'We got a lot of work done at Marissa's. She phoned me this morning to say the earthquake was a good sign — things were moving. She's a bit fey that way, Marissa, believes in signs and instincts.'

Margaret couldn't tell whether Chrissie was trying to be annoying or conciliatory. Probably Chrissie didn't know either. She, too, had noticed the intensity between Charles and Ernie, wondering how serious it was. Margaret bent down to scratch Slocum's ear, grateful that some relationships were simple and steady and predictable.

'I got another letter from Janey,' she offered.

'Oh, yes?' Chrissie asked.

'She's coming for a couple of weeks. I knew she would get tired of that Canadian tundra.'

'Just make sure she comes *after* our trip to Hawaii,' said Chrissie.

'Of course,' Margaret nodded, pleased at Chrissie's concern. 'I told her about it months ago.'

Chrissie considered how much she needed a vacation, how tired she was. Immediately she released the thought, afraid she might lose all momentum.

'Hawaii,' came a voice from behind Chrissie. Like a disembodied TV announcer. Or a ghost. 'You two city girls won't last a week in all that peace. Especially you,' Douglas pointed his pipe stem at Chrissie. 'Ocean breezes. Palm trees. Luaus. You'll go batty.'

'Balmy,' suggested Ernie.

Chrissie wasn't laughing. Maybe she *had* come to rely on this neon racket as an artificial pulse. She remembered when Jacqueline, who used to cashier at the El Cortez Hotel, came down for a visit. 'How can you stand all this noise?' she had asked. 'Noise, what noise?' Chrissie had answered. 'The screeching bus wheels and never-ending construction work,' Jacqueline had retorted. Maybe she had gone deaf. No, no, when she had visited Jacqueline in Mendocino, she nearly went mad from the silent evenings. She realized that the horns and sirens were a sort of company.

'You may be right,' she finally answered Douglas. 'I remember Mendocino and how those damn birds drove me crazy in the morning.'

'You slept through the earthquake today,' Ernie reminded her.

'Of course, there's a larger question,' said Douglas, barely suppressing his grin. Margaret noticed that Douglas never looked so cheerful as when he was teasing Chrissie. 'How will the city function without you? I can see the headlines now: CHRISSIE MACINNES ON VACATION. SF CLOSES DOWN.'

'You'll be sorry, Mr Sinclair,' Chrissie said. 'It's your news shop that will be missing us. And yourself.'

She looked over for Ernie's agreement, but he was polishing a smudge off Charles Hunter's badge.

The Borodin Quartet played furiously from Douglas's office. They struck a particularly high note which repeated and repeated. Douglas marched to the back of the shop.

'Enough of this.' Chrissie threw her hands in the air. 'I've got a hundred errands, including the dreaded old laundry –, before my shift this afternoon. See you all. Maybe at canvassing tomorrow?' She looked directly at Margaret, who was concentrating on the symmetry of magazines on a far shelf. 'See some of you, anyway,' said Chrissie, walking heavily from the shop.

Outside, cold wind raced, slapping around the corners. In the alley, a drunken woman huddled close inside her soiled raincoat. Chrissie raised her hand in greeting. Three or four regulars just on this block. She remembered her arguments with Margaret about these people. Margaret couldn't understand why they didn't go to hostels for the night. There was food, warmth, a bed. Why would people choose the street? Independence, Chrissie had argued. Lenore, in her Daly City security, probably thought of her and Margaret as street people, living downtown when they both could be retired on social security at the senior home. Margaret rejected the comparison. She didn't consider these people who huddled their nights against air vents as part of the neighborhood. She didn't regard them as living here. Because they didn't pay rent? Och, she just didn't understand. Margaret didn't condemn the street people. She felt sorry for them, which Chrissie reckoned was worse.

Chrissie hurried along the pavement. She would never get the laundry done at this rate. Douglas was right about Hawaii, damn him. She would miss the city. But she surely wouldn't miss this wind. The older she got, the more wind summoned her ethnic heritage, bad lungs. She could barely make it up these hills. She didn't know what would kill her – bronchitis, pneumonia, emphysema, tuberculosis – but she was sure it would be some British lung disorder triggered by the damn San Francisco wind. Chrissie liked to pose as indestructible, with her sturdy step and firm shoulders. Few people knew the internal frailties. As Gudrun once said, 'They'll put your frame in a museum, *"Homo Scottus"*.' Chrissie hadn't bothered to tell her that she had already willed her body to UC Medical Center.

Across the street, she saw Mrs Winchester (such a fierce one, out and about at ninety-two) struggling against the wind in her walker. On her own side of the pavement, twenty paces ahead, Chrissie watched a blond (German?) tourist carrying a Lufthansa bag from one shoulder and three heavy cameras over his belly. She had met him at Mummer's last night. He told her proudly that he had found a room for nineteen dollars a week. She tried not to worry about him displaying all that wealth in the Tenderloin.

Why the sour mood, she asked herself. The wind? The earthquake? Margaret and Bentman? The election? All that was enough, but Chrissie suspected it was because of her laundry. She hated doing laundry. Hated the roach spray that laced the washroom. Shivered, thinking about the time she opened the dryer to find an army of tiny, jerking creatures. Margaret had laughed at her — 'Afraid of those little things?' — delighted that for once she was more worldy than her friend.

'Morning, Miss MacInnes.' Chrissie was startled back to primary school when the principal had said, 'Morning Miss MacInnes,' returning her to the multiplication tables. No one called her 'Miss MacInnes' any more. Most people didn't even know her last name. She looked up tentatively, into the face of Kevin Sinclair. They had almost collided. Of course, that's why he greeted her. And the 'Miss MacInnes'? He had called her that as a boy.

'Morning, Kevin,' she said evenly, without false warmth. God, he was always such a twit. Stealing from Little Pete's tin when he was a kid, getting kicked out of City College for cheating. Why should she be surprised he wound up on the side of a thug like Carson? She knew that Kevin didn't like her either. Once she overheard him asking Margaret why Chrissie wasn't a lady like herself. Why was she such a tough broad? Tough broad, Chrissie had smiled. It was the biggest compliment she got that week.

They passed without another word. Chrissie wondered what commotion he would cause at the shop. Such a morning! Kevin. Earthquake. Margaret's romance. Doing the laundry always sunk her in a stinking mood.

When Kevin opened the glass door, Margaret's first reaction was relief that Chrissie had already left. One conflict avoided. She glanced cautiously at Douglas, but he was deep in *The Wall Street Journal.* Kevin walked right up to Charles and Ernie. They seemed friendly enough. One thing she admired about Ernie was that despite his support for Marissa, he could remain civil with the other side. He got along with everyone, with Chrissie, Mr Poulos, Douglas, Kevin. Douglas had complained that Kevin and Ernie were friendly because they had a mutual interest — albeit a different taste — in pornography. He said that Charles was probably receiving some kind of bribe from Carson. Margaret dismissed this cantankerousness. Douglas never had a kind word for anyone associating with his son.

'Three weeks to go and Carson has it clinched.' Kevin spoke loudly enough to provoke his father.

Margaret watched Kevin play with his dark moustache, such an anomaly against the sandy Sinclair hair.

'Hang on,' said Ernie. 'This is a democracy. People are innocent until proven guilty. Candidates are candidates until elected.'

'No,' said Douglas. 'This is capitalism, where the guilty extort their way to innocence and candidates invest in victory.'

Margaret wished she could still be shocked at their arguing in public. She understood that the shop was home to both men. That's probably why Kevin had such a hard time moving. She suspected that she and the regulars like Ernie had become an easy alternative to family.

Charles stared down at his highly polished black oxfords as if searching for a reassuring reflection.

'If you're implying something . . .' Kevin looked directly at his father.

Margaret often wondered what tied them together besides this hatred. It was as though the boy had fought even against

120

physical resemblance. In contrast to Douglas's understated sweaters and slacks, Kevin dressed like a carnival barker in his gaudy striped suits and flowered shirts. What could you expect from a boy without a mother? She checked herself. Probably some woman in Alaska was looking at Rob right now in his ragged Pendleton shirts and asking what kind of mother *he* had.

'I'm not *implying* anything.' Douglas slowly folded the newspaper and set it back on the rack. He knew that his son was infuriated by precision and he made sure that the paper was creaseless before he continued. 'I'm saying Jake Carson is a crook, that he's being supported by the dregs of city business and that he's going to buy his way to the top. With the help of my son.'

'I've grown up, Dad, in case you hadn't noticed.'

'You'll always be my son.' Douglas sounded resigned. 'Just as you'll always be using that office upstairs. Some things never change.'

Kevin's face revealed shock, then belligerence. 'I've been planning to move out.' His voice gained strength. 'I've got a nice piece of property on Larkin, with a big office upstairs.'

Margaret thought she saw Douglas blanche. Sometimes a hint of frailty would cross his jaw. He usually recovered quickly. 'I imagine you have several "nice pieces of property". Where's this one? Over one of your adult bookstores?'

'It's a free world,' said Kevin. 'The First Amendment, you may remember, protects freedom of speech.'

'Well, if you aren't the clever civics professor today.' Douglas tightened. 'You might start thinking about your responsibilities as well as your rights. You've never done a thing that wasn't for yourself. Most of the time that's been okay. Until now, you haven't directly harmed anyone.'

'Where do you think I learned to look out for myself?' Kevin shouted. 'Growing up in this neighborhood. In the middle of the city. With a father who was more concerned with the price of . . .'

'What do you think I did with that money? Play the horses? It went to —'

'— to care for a motherless boy,' Kevin droned in a horrible caricature of his father.

Margaret stroked Slocum with her stockinged feet. How she enjoyed the dog's long, wagging, friendly body.

Charles stepped back toward the door. Fear took a fleeting path through Ernie's eyes. Then he recouped his usual affability. 'Hey, guys.' He moved between father and son. 'You don't want to duke it out in front of the lady.'

Kevin stared at Douglas with new will. Douglas glared at Ernie.

'I've got work to do.' Kevin patted his leather briefcase and marched toward the stairway.

'A shame on his mother,' Douglas muttered. 'A curse on his father.' He shuffled toward the back of the shop.

'So much for King Lear.' Ernie shrugged to Margaret and reached over the counter to pat Slocum who was wide-eyed, surveying the commotion. 'Great day, eh?'

'And only eleven o'clock,' said Margaret, straining for cheerfulness. 'What's next?'

'Well, I could lose my flower sitter.' Ernie looked nervously at his watch and then regretfully at Charles.

'I'll walk you there,' Charles offered. 'I should be going myself.'

'Bye, Margaret.'

'See you later, Margaret.'

'Well, pooch,' Margaret rubbed Slocum's cool nose gently, 'we'd better stick together. I'm beginning to think the only peaceful communication is inter-species.'

She glanced at the photographs of the three children. She knew they loved her. Yes, Chrissie was right reminding her how often Rob phoned. And Janey not only wrote letters, but she had done those poems about her 'struggles'. The girl had always romanticized trouble. Okay, quitting school and raising Sylvia wasn't her first choice, but they had had some good fun. Sometimes it was like playing house. Besides, Margaret knew that she had been lucky, in her own way, to have a job during the Depression and to move up to the Cornucopia Restaurant. Lucky to have met handsome Bill Sawyer and to bear his three — no, Chrissie corrected, 'our three' — children. Life could have been a lot worse. As much as Margaret was touched by Janey trying to understand, she resented the 'struggle' interpretation of her history. After all, it was *her* history. No, she could *not* say 'herstory'.

She didn't notice him until he spoke. Speaking wasn't exactly the right term. Coughing. He was coughing to announce himself.

'Oh.' Margaret felt unaccountably annoyed at being torn from the family like this. 'Good morning.'

'Morning,' he grudged.

'How are you today?' she asked almost defiantly. She realized how selfconscious she had become about his aloofness these last few weeks. Every few days, he would drop by and cough and then wait for the package. The package. Where had she put it? Just a minute now. Why was she trembling? He was just a kid, an ignorant kid. Never so much as a 'Good morning' or a 'Goodbye'.

He leaned over the counter. 'Just fine,' he said.

Slocum growled. He glared. She growled again.

Margaret patted Slocum. As she tried to reassure the dog her anger rose. She wondered why she had wanted him to talk.

'The book is here, somewhere.' She rummaged around the shelf. Had Kevin given her a book this morning? She didn't remember. Because of the fight. And the earthquake. She felt exhausted. Oh, had Kevin given her that stupid book or not?

The young man shifted from one foot to the other.

Slocum growled again. Reaching over to calm the dog, Margaret knocked her half-empty coffee cup on the pile of *New York Times*. 'Damn.'

The man squinted through pale eyelashes, then looked at his watch. 'I don't know what happened, mam, but I have to leave. Will you tell Mr Sinclair if he has a book for my mother today, he can deliver it on his own.'

Slocum barked as he walked out the door. Alarmed by the noise, Douglas hurried from the back of the shop. He called, 'Margaret, Margaret, are you all right, Margaret?'

The young man had gone before Douglas reached the counter.

'Who was that?' He noticed the soggy newspapers.

'I don't know.' Margaret was unwilling to implicate Kevin. 'Someone who upset Slocum and then I upset the coffee. Oh, dear.'

'Sounds like we've had enough upsets this morning. You

look a little tired. Why don't you knock off early, Margaret, catch some of that sun. It's going to be pouring rain by the end of the week.'

Margaret nodded wearily, no thought of protest.

An hour later, she was sipping her third cup of tea at home and eating a taste of cottage cheese with her graham crackers. She would take a walk in the sun as Douglas had instructed, a walk around Union Square, but first she needed some solitude. Often she wondered how she had lived so many years with other people. Pop and Mom and Sylvia in the tiny flat and then the boarding-house room with Sylvia and then the apartment with Bill and the kids. Sometimes she felt she hadn't properly grown up until her own children left home. She hadn't been independent until the age of fifty.

Looking around the studio now, she thought how much she first hated being on her own. Petrified, she had been on constant guard against rapists and burglars. She would check under the bed two or three times a night. She left a hallway light burning. Then she realized that since the Murphy bed had been in the wall all day, there couldn't possibly be anyone hiding beneath it. And because of the street lights, she didn't need the hallway lamp. Gradually, she had come to enjoy living alone. Knowing that she could return to the studio the way she had left it. Knowing that her mess wouldn't disturb anyone. Knowing that she could close the door on all the comings and goings and gossip and worry and electioneering and feuding and bustle of a life which she loved but from which she needed respite. Neighborhood people were always organizing events for seniors. OK for others, but she had had enough people on the outside and more than enough people still on the inside — plenty of things to work out in her heart with Pop and Sylvia and Bill and Janey and the others.

A phone rang. Faintly. Margaret hoped that it was from Mrs Winchester's apartment. No, there it was again. She checked the domed clock. Twelve-fifteen. A whole hour gone. This was her normal break. It could be anyone. Roger. Probably Roger. He had taken to ringing each afternoon, just to stay in touch. She worried about what Roger wanted. No, quite honestly, she knew what he wanted. A home.

Marriage. For years now, that's what she had longed for. Yet just a minute ago, she was savoring her solitude. What would it be like to live with someone again? Even someone as considerate as Roger. Was he strong enough? What would it feel like to be someone's wife? The phone continued ringing. Maybe she wouldn't answer it. Then he would worry. See, already they were tied. She was accountable for her time. Responsible not to get knifed or run over or lost. Now, it would be legitimate for her to be away. She could be shopping or having coffee with Mrs Winchester or doing any of a dozen things, but the truth was, she sat right here listening to the phone ring. Again. How could she explain that she had sat, letting it ring? Again.

'Hello?' she spoke softly, stretching for her own tenderness.

'Hello, Margaret.' He named her. Strange tone.

'Yes.' She still tried for brightness.

'This is Kevin.'

She felt relieved and disappointed. Then, suddenly, she remembered the red-haired man. The book.

'Margaret, Mrs Hartley's son called me.'

'Yes, I know.' She sighed heavily. 'I meant to tell you. But I left early because your father, because the morning got so chaotic.'

'Margaret,' he cut across her words, 'where is the book?'

'Did you give it to me, oh, yes, of course you did, very early today.'

'Margaret, what's got into you? Would you like me to come over so we can talk about this?'

Her cheeks burned. What had got into *him*? So stern, cold. She didn't care for his tone, no, not at all. Then, as if fear illumined her memory, she saw the book on the back shelf, with the special order magazines. She told him that was where it must be.

'Well, I'm right here at the counter,' he spoke doubtfully. 'Let me check.'

She heard him shuffling and was overcome by some incomprehensible terror until he said, 'Yes.' She could hear him relax. 'It's right here,' and then, as if conjuring the spirit of the package, he added, 'Mrs Hartley had especially requested this one.'

Margaret had wanted to know why he left a different book each time rather than sending a pile at once. Her passing discomfort at the routine now materialized in questions. Why didn't Kevin visit the poor woman, himself? How could someone so sick read so much? But the Kevin at the other end of the line was not the familiar Kevin to whom she could ask such questions.

'Hmmm,' he dismissed the minor misunderstanding, 'I'll drop off this one myself. See you soon, Margaret. Thanks.'

Eighteen

Kevin smiled expansively the next morning as he presented Margaret with a gardenia as well as the small brown package. Margaret sensed a mutual reprieve. Still, she didn't understand these book rituals. Last night she had wanted to consult Roger, however he got so romantic with the candles and champagne. It was the wrong time. Then he started talking about his grand schemes and they had both been carried away.

Margaret reminded herself to return Kevin's smile, to thank him for the gardenia. Damn sinus. Sweet boy.

'Nice day.' Kevin seemed unhurried about returning to work. Margaret knew Douglas would be arriving any moment. She couldn't cope with a fight today. She wanted to reflect on the pleasures of last night. She wanted to rest.

'Storm coming,' said Margaret, setting her sore feet on Slocum's back.

'Corns again?' smiled Kevin.

'Afraid so,' answered Margaret, searching his grin for the boy she used to know. Chrissie called her wide-eyed because she looked for good memories in people. Still, it was better than being sour as Chrissie, herself, pretended to be.

The door swung open. '*Buenos Dias,*' called Roberto, opening the door with his foot, juggling two cups of coffee and a bag of pastries. He blew his long black hair out of his eyes.

When Roberto noticed Kevin, his face sank. 'Morning,' he said dismissively, then turned to Margaret. 'Bearclaws!' he declared. Sweetness seeped from the white bag. 'To celebrate,' he winked.

'Why, thank you,' Margaret was slightly nauseated by the heavy aroma of almond and vanilla. Why were they always bringing her things? Did they think she needed charity? Chrissie told her not to complain. She represented the archetypal mother and they were all making recompense. Chrissie and her psychology extension courses! Well, perhaps

127

the idea pleased Margaret a little.

'Celebrate what?' Kevin demanded nervously.

Roberto ignored him. Fastidiously, he unsnapped the plastic lids from the styrofoam cups. He knew how careful Margaret was about her counter.

'Election news?' Kevin persisted.

Roberto stiffened. The two men faced each other with wintry shoulders. Kevin moved back, almost imperceptibly. Roberto shrugged, as if exorcising himself. 'Nope. Love news. The pursuit of happiness.' He toasted Margaret with his coffee, '*Felicidades*.'

Kevin's face showed confusion, annoyance and then belligerence. He stood stoically on the edge of their breakfast. Margaret knew she shouldn't invite Kevin to join them, but she couldn't help the reflex. Extending her pastry to him, she noticed his jaw tighten. She didn't need to look over her shoulder to know that Douglas Sinclair was coming, walking at his quick clip, past the drugstore, toward the shop.

'So, Margaret,' Kevin ignored Roberto. 'It's been great talking with you. Bye for now.' He went up to his office.

Margaret sometimes imagined that she lived in a world of her own construction because the characters didn't speak to each other, didn't even acknowledge each other. Did Chrissie see Roger? Did Douglas see Kevin? Perhaps they had never been in the same room together. Perhaps she had created all of them.

'Morning, Roberto,' said Douglas. Margaret relaxed. At least *they* communicated. Douglas broke off a piece of Roberto's pastry.

'Hey, man,' Roberto protested.

'Inflation.' Douglas licked the stickiness from his teeth. 'Just accept the metaphor. We're all losing corners off our incomes.'

'Except Carson,' said Roberto.

'Oh, you heard that too?' asked Douglas.

'Can't prove it yet.' Roberto turned to Margaret. 'But there's something fishy about Carson's accounts.'

Margaret sighed, thinking this was just what Chrissie had said all along.

'A little at a time,' said Douglas, 'apparently in cash. Less

128

risk of detection that way. Clever.'

'Maybe not clever enough,' said Roberto.

Margaret recalled the redhead; the young aide at the TV debate — it was becoming such a spiral — the commotion about Mrs Hartley's book; Kevin's face this morning. No, she must stop this suspicion. She was caught in a whirlpool. That's what imagination did to you. Imagination was why she had worried too much as a child.

'Don't look so troubled, Margaret,' Douglas admonished. 'You always knew there were good guys and bad guys.'

'*Si*, you could get arrested for looking that nervous.' Roberto had caught Douglas's high spirits.

'Right,' answered Margaret, reaching down absently toward Slocum, who licked her hand. 'I haven't been myself lately.'

'Don't we know.' Roberto's eyes widened.

As eager as Margaret was to avoid the topic of Roger, especially in front of Douglas, she was glad to be moving away from the election. What business of hers was this bribery anyway? And what business of theirs was her involvement with Roger? Sometimes she did wish she had imagined the whole circus.

Chrissie was listening to Gudrun talk. Listening to the rhythm of her Swinglish, the music of lilts and lows. It was the second morning this week they had spent together at Manning's Cafeteria. Chrissie wondered if Gudrun's Swedish accent were more interesting than her ideas. Still, they were old friends, and she could talk with Gudrun about things she couldn't even say to Margaret. Recently Gudrun had been more available than Margaret, not having a Unitarian minister in her bed. Chrissie felt guilty about exploiting Gudrun's friendship. But she had been good to Gudrun after Nils died, staying up with her all night, holding back the pill bottle, hiding her for a few days when one of her johns got too persistent. Friendship didn't have to be a steady deposit. It was more crucial at certain times. So, she asked herself, why did she feel deserted by Margaret?

'Christina, come to Wilbur Hot Springs with me. You get this trouble off your soul — the election, Margaret. You come back your old self.'

'Crikey, Gudrun.' Chrissie set down her coffee mug. Pitiful Mannings coffee, it tasted like molasses and acid. 'You act like "this trouble" is an emotional state. You act like the Tenderloin will be better when I feel better. Forget the election?'

'Yah, in a certain way, yah.' Gudrun buttered her rubbery muffin. 'You live here. You are one of the influences. If you feel better, if you give off the aura of —'

'Spare me, love,' said Chrissie. 'Keep that "aura" business for your self-absorbed guru friends.'

'Tell me who is self-absorbed? Who thinks she is Jesus Christ?' Gudrun was uncommonly provoked. 'All I say is that you ruin your health with late night meetings and endless anxiety. Who does that help? Fine to be involved. Not fine to be swallowed. I don't say be self-indulgent. I just say understand you can't run this place by yourself. Have some ... humility.'

'I'm not doing anything by myself.' Chrissie was exasperated. 'Ernie, he's involved. Roberto. Douglas. And let's not forget Marissa.'

Gudrun's pretty face revealed the bored frustration she often felt with Chrissie's politics. She rubbed the turquoise on her Navajo bracelet.

'You're just love-sick,' she said. 'Just jealous of Holy Roger.'

'What do you mean?' Chrissie shifted uncomfortably. She glanced at two gay men, deep in conversation. This gay business was all very well for Ernie. And maybe for Charles. However why did they have to assume she was also that way? Couldn't you support something without doing it? Gudrun had some pretty fantastical ideas, but this was the limit.

'You're jealous of Bentman because you love Margaret,' Gudrun grinned.

'As a friend.' Chrissie cleared her throat.

'As a friend,' conceded Gudrun. 'You don't have to go to bed with someone to be in love.'

'Friendship is a fine word. Don't use phrases like "in love".'

'Why not?'

'Because they get misinterpreted.' Chrissie stared at her hands, at the wrinkles gathering between the fingers.

'Misinterpret, exactly,' said Gudrun, 'what you do with

130

Margaret. You haven't lost her. How long has she known you? Decades. She loves you, Chrissie, more than she could ever love the preacher. She loves you and Slocum.'

'Thanks,' Chrissie grimaced.

'*Var så god.*'

'So let's get back to the election.' Chrissie raised her voice. 'Are you coming canvassing or not?'

'Ja, sure, tomorrow night. If you come to the hot springs with me this weekend.'

'Can't,' said Chrissie, distracted by the time and agitated by Gudrun's persistent physicality. 'I've got the Nicaragua benefit. And tutoring on Saturday morning.'

'So you schedule your love?' Gudrun looked amused.

'What are you talking about now?'

'It doesn't get out of hand that way. All your good work, all your love, all so well-organized.'

'Love. Tutoring. What do you mean? Once a week with the Binh family. Big deal. English is a tough language. You know. *I* know — for a year after I arrived no one could understand me. What does it have to do with love?'

Gudrun shook her head and played with a curl behind her ear. 'Sometimes I think part of your heart is closed.'

'I don't expect people to love me for my political work.' Frustrated, Chrissie dug into her pocket for a tip. 'I don't expect . . .'

'No,' Gudrun sighed, 'I don't expect that you expect anything.'

Margaret knew she had no right to solitude on her job. She wasn't being paid to meditate. But she was delighted when Roberto and Douglas finally left. So many things to think about. One of the best parts of aging for her had been the way choices seemed to lessen. Decreased mobility, duty and possibility were as reassuring to her as they were maddening to Chrissie. Chrissie seemed to be generated by frenzy as much as she, herself, was sustained by quiet. Another benefit to growing older, you could see there were different kinds of truth. The walls were more flexible and that was okay. You didn't need to lean against external structures to test reality. You knew you existed. You knew you would continue to exist until it was time to go. Chrissie, however, was still testing the walls, like some metaphysical surveyor. And she was always building new ones.

Margaret sighed, thinking how peace had been shattered during the last few weeks. Roger riding in on his white horse. Chrissie getting more and more wound up in the election. Kevin and Douglas escalating their combat. Ernie falling in love with Charles. And the red-haired fellow collecting books. Margaret had always known there was something peculiar about the arrangement. She even dreamed about it last week. Now there was more talk about bribery. No, she insisted to herself, Kevin would never get involved in something as seedy as that. He would never get her involved. Still, passing small amounts of money in the books would be less hazardous than transferring a large bundle at midnight somewhere. And she would be the perfect channel. Who would suspect Margaret Sawyer? No, she insisted to herself again, she was getting carried away. She detested this election business. The violence. The arguments. The hatred. Three more weeks. Could she survive three weeks?

Kevin had left his package right on top of the pile of *New York Times.* Right out in the open for anyone to find, a brown paper bag, Scotch-taped shut. Hardly the way bribes were conducted. You could get years in jail for bribery and election fraud. Don't be ridiculous, she told herself. Bribery was committed through car windows in the darkness. Not out in the open.

She slipped the package beneath the counter, tucking it on the lower shelf, safe, so Mrs Dougal or Captain George wouldn't pick it up inadvertently.

Hawaii, they would be going to Hawaii when it was all over, Margaret reminded herself. She thought about palm trees and cocktails served in pineapple shells. Quite honestly, she wasn't all that keen on exotic travels. Chrissie had talked her into the expedition. Margaret suggested they might have fun staying in San Francisco for their two weeks off, pretending to be tourists. Chrissie told her she had no sense of adventure. Margaret thought about Janey and Rob and Michael and suspected Chrissie was correct.

Still, San Francisco fascinated her after all these years. She couldn't imagine Europe as any more exciting. North Beach pasta and espresso. The Green Valley Restaurant where you used to be able to get an entire family-style meal for one dollar and fifty cents. Or was it two dollars and fifty cents? And the Marina, sitting on one of those benches at the Marina watching kite flyers and joggers and scanning beyond the bay to the sensuous Marin hills. San Francisco was so bright and diverse. Take the Mission. Beautiful brown-eyed children. Spiffy lowriders cruising in those wild — and often reckless — cars. Even the Tenderloin was fascinating sometimes. The parade of immigrants. Women her age from Europe — like Brigid at the Yum Yum Room or Gudrun and Chrissie waiting tables at Mummer's. Then, a little younger, a little further down on the totem pole of jobs, were the black women from Chicago or the South. And still younger, working in the kitchens, were the Asians and Latinas. Of course, as Roberto pointed out, there was discrimination in hiring, so it wasn't always according to age or seniority. But Margaret thought she saw a pattern of progress that drew new people here and made the Tenderloin quite cosmopolitan. Just as interesting as Hawaii, anyway.

Margaret leaned against the back of the stool and closed her eyes. She knew Chrissie was right, knew it would be healthy to get away. The distance would do them both good. It would give her perspective. About Roger, for instance. What on earth was she going to do? He said he didn't want to rush her. She had heard these words, but she had also seen how his eyes held the frailty of lost time and possible loneliness. Yes, it would be good to get away from all this, to be with Chrissie as in the old days: laughing, arguing, gossiping, without the pressure of this past month.

The shop had grown too quiet. From outside, the honking and screeching spoke of a distant, unfriendly world. She reached down to hug Slocum for company, but the dog looked so peaceful that Margaret felt she had no right to disturb her sleep. Surfacing to the counter, she passed Kevin's parcel. A wave of fear ran across her shoulders. How could she be so frightened of her old friend? Of a boy who was almost her son? Certainly, she should trust him. She knew it was her own weak-kneed worrying which led her to the next unprincipled step.

Margaret took advantage of her solitude to remove the package from the shelf. A quick glance at the book inside would exonerate Kevin. In her nervousness, she tore part of the bag with the tape. A small rip; she could repair it without problem. Such was fear. She felt more than that. Guilty. She was a common thief, a wife steaming open her husband's letters. How could she respect herself? Nimbly, she continued.

The book slid from the bag, as evenly as if she burgled every day. Agatha Christie, sure enough, *Death On The Nile.* One of her favorites. She recalled figuring out who did it, halfway through, sticking to her opinion, which she usually couldn't do, and finding out she had been right all along. Margaret felt light-headed with relief. Dizzily, she noticed that the book felt bulky at the front. From an envelope inside. Enough, she warned herself. Bad enough to doubt Kevin. Here was proof of his goodwill right in her hands. Why did she persist? It would be so easy to ignore the long envelope. Probably a get well card. But she couldn't help herself. Inside, she found hundred dollar bills, one, two, five of them.

Behind her, Margaret heard someone approach the door. Please god it wasn't Mrs Hartley's son or whoever-the-hell that fellow was. Please God this was . . .'

'Hi, cutie,' she heard Ernie's voice. 'Dead quiet in here.' He bent forward to kiss her. She leaned to the side lest he look in her lap.

'Coy today?' He was startled by her demureness.

Margaret was anxious to get rid of Ernie before Mrs Hartley's son arrived. Such a fool she was. Why couldn't she leave well enough alone? What business of hers was the election, or Kevin's behavior for that matter? He was a grown man.

She picked up the feather mop and dusted Ernie's nose. Somewhat surprised by her own presence of mind, she said, 'It's just this awful cold. I don't want to spread it.'

'Communicable diseases are my specialty,' said Ernie.

Margaret laughed in spite of herself. This relaxed her enough to think of a way out. 'Ernie, could I ask a favor?'

'The moon,' he smiled flirtatiously.

'A cup of coffee?' she parried, noticing how astonished he was at her asking a favor. 'It's the cold. I don't know how I'll stay awake through the morning.' She spoke more quietly so Douglas would not hear. Oh, God, that's all she needed – the two of them gossiping and her with bribery (is that what this was?) in her lap.

'Sure.' He responded to the urgency in her tone. Halfway out the door, he turned back. 'Cream and sugar?'

Margaret stared at him, somewhat dazed. 'Pardon?'

He frowned, 'Are you okay?'

'Cream and sugar.' His words echoed from a crevice in her brain.

'No,' she said. 'I mean, yes, both, thank you.'

'Sure,' he shrugged.

Hastily, Margaret put the envelope back in the book. Then the damn thing wouldn't fit in the bag. The brown paper ripped slightly as she forced it. She stopped, set everything on her lap and inhaled sharply. Relax, she told herself. She tried again. This time it fit. She slipped the book under the counter and turned her duster to the cigarette case before Ernie returned.

'You look better already,' said Ernie. 'A caffeine addict. Never would have suspected you, Margaret.'

'Who knows where darkness lurks?'

'I'd be surprised if there was much in you,' he joked. 'As for me, I'm a walking model of human weakness. Charming as that can be. Why, last night, Charles and I . . .' he stopped as recognition registered on her face.

'I thought something was happening.' She felt revived by the coffee.

'We have to keep it from his macho buddies on the force.'

Margaret nodded. She reflected back to fifteen years before when she had met Ernie. How cold and brittle she had been toward this queer fellow. And how he had melted her fears. 'But if Charles's buddies only understood,' she smirked, 'they'd be so happy for you.'

Ernie raised his cup, 'Cheers.'

'Cheers to –' Margaret was interrupted by the cold wind and Mrs Hartley's son.

Ernie saw Margaret shiver. 'Hey, are you feeling okay?'

'Yes,' she stiffened and pivoted to the young man. 'Good morning. How is your mother today?' She heard her voice,

135

high and reedy.

'Better,' he answered curtly.

Margaret could see how uncomfortable he was with the masquerade.

'Well, Kevin left her another book,' she said cheerfully, reaching to the shelf.

Slocum awoke and stood with her paws on the counter, nuzzling toward Ernie. She looked over at the other man and growled.

'Down, girl,' said Ernie, who didn't much like the stranger's attitude. 'You've got to be diplomatic working with the public.'

Margaret tried to laugh and to soothe Slocum at the same time.

The young man tapped his foot impatiently.

'Why, here it is.' She listened to her words whine above them.

'Thanks.' he almost grabbed the parcel.

At the same time, they both noticed that the tape was unsealed.

He looked at her. She looked down. Then, as quietly as he had entered, Mrs Hartley's son left the shop.

Nineteen

Margaret found herself walking down Powell Street to Woolworth's after work, even though she had told Roger she could be reached at home this afternoon. She needed to distract herself from this anger and fear about Kevin. And she had a terrible yen for pizza pie. Perhaps she went to Woolworth's for the company as much as for the pizza. Janey used to complain that the atmosphere was tacky. People crowded and pushed to buy junk that would break or rip or crack in four weeks. Anyway, she said, what was the point when you could get something almost as cheap at a Macy's sale? Yes, it was true that there were many items Margaret wouldn't buy at Woolworth's. Yes, she did keep an eye open for sales at Liberty House and even Roos Atkins. But some things were best here. The lipstick, for instance. Margaret also told Janey that Woolworth's brought back New York memories. And the Macy's here wasn't even the same company as the Macy's in New York.

The lipstick counter was always changing with new colors and shines. Margaret searched for her shade of red. So much purple nowadays. Still, it was better than those ghostly pales they sold when Janey was a teenager. All that white lipstick! Even though Woolworth's stocked the fancy new lip glosses, they had — for the last thirty years — also carried her color of red. Here it was. Compared to most items, the price hadn't gone up much. At this same counter, she could always find Pond's cold cream.

The lipstick counter. They found her here after the telegram about Michael. Chrissie had known where to look. Sure, enough, she was at the lipstick counter, inspecting different shades. The tears ran down her cheeks into a horrid orange coral. Good thing that Chrissie had thought to check Woolworth's. The saleswomen were getting panicky about their weepy customer. One clerk showed great relief when Chrissie

137

took Margaret's arm and expressed sympathy when Chrissie whispered something about a death in the family. Today, Margaret's decisions were quick and clear, one red lipstick and one jar of cold cream.

'Forget the pepper?' Marty turned halfway from the pizza oven and smiled at Margaret.

'Right, the usual. I like pepper, but it doesn't like me.'

Suddenly there was a queue behind her. Maybe not suddenly. Maybe she just noticed it. Marty had no time for chat. Too many elbows. Too many specials, no anchovies.

So, despite the wind, Margaret walked out to Market Street, eating her pizza. The cheese was soft and stringy and it seemed to stiffen in the wind. At moments like this, on the edge of cold, the smell of tomato paste and mozzarella steaming in her face, Margaret might just as well be back in Manhattan. No, New York pizza was better, with more spice and thicker crust. Was this nostalgia? You had to watch for nostalgia as you grew older. The past seemed to be better, when, in fact, it had only been different. And maybe not all that different. A tug on her purse. Or at least Margaret thought so. Pulling it back, she turned to see a young man ducking into the crowd. Her imagination? His timidity? Margaret couldn't tell, but she was grateful now, the purse tucked safely under her arm and the pizza still warm in her hands.

Agatha Christie intruded before the next bite. Who could she talk to? Chrissie, yes, but she would be furious with her for passing on so many books and bribes. Margaret supposed they were bribes. Chrissie would get Kevin arrested before she even bothered to ask his side of the story. Margaret was sure that in some way Kevin had been tricked into this business.

Roger, she could also tell Roger. But she was as much afraid of what Roger wouldn't say as of what Chrissie would say. What was wrong with her? Why couldn't she talk to her closest friends? She worried about their protectiveness, leery that it would get her into deeper trouble. Afraid. What was all this nonsense anyway? She would just have to speak with Kevin. Perhaps there was a simple explanation. It was better for him to know she knew — whatever it was she did know —

than for him to go on guessing. Fresh air, she sighed. Always good for the brain. She crumpled the greasy wax paper and tossed it in a wire litter basket. Turning back in the direction of Geary Street, Margaret wondered whether Chrissie was right about politics — that it touched everyone, no matter how much you minded your own business. The wind was rising and it looked as if it might rain any minute.

Chrissie sat in the rocker and worried.

This wasn't her usual recreation, not when winter threatened at any moment. It wasn't her usual way of worrying. Normally she would confront the problem. But what was the problem? She felt anxious. About Margaret, yes, but what about Margaret? Something was going on besides this palaver with Bentman. Margaret had been cold, completely unreachable these last few days.

Who knows, maybe this was what happened to women in the throes of romance. A romance with Roger Bentman! After that dopey printer and George Lemington III, why did she expect her friend to have better taste? Chrissie's rocker faced the mirror, an instrument toward which she made no pretensions. However, this morning Chrissie had been avoiding her own glance. She stood now, accepting the weight on her sturdy legs, and approached the mirror.

She started at the top. Grey hair growing greyer. The change was obvious because the hairnet was a shade darker than her curls. Tomorrow, she would pick up a new net. Next she examined her face. Character. Mama had always seen character in Chrissie's face. The heavy eyebrows; the straight nose; the serious eyes. Character. Rajid had seen beauty. So he said. No, no false modesty — Chrissie had seen her beauty reflected back in his dark eyes. Everyone wants that kind of mirror, Chrissie understood that.

She poured another cup of tea and returned to the rocker. Enough sentiment. What about friendship? Wasn't friendship still valuable to Margaret? Why couldn't Margaret find 'affirmation', as Ernie would say, in her love? Margaret knew that Chrissie loved her, didn't she? How much was three decades of friendship worth compared to the promise of Prince Valiant? Really, that woman was too fantastical for her own good. What was love? Understanding? Constancy? And who would choose Roger Bentman over Chrissie MacInnes? Margaret probably thought a choice wasn't necessary. But Chrissie knew better and she could tell from Bentman's expression that he knew too.

What if Gudrun were right about her 'scheduling' love? She hated it when criticism brought this kind of chilly self-doubt. The rocking grew furious. So what was wrong with being organized? Political work was constructive. Other relationships were so mutable, so susceptible to frigid headaches and cold feet and weak egos. Tutoring on Saturday mornings wasn't much of a contribution. However there was value in that sort of reliability, in a 'love' which answers needs rather than seeks self-reflection. She cared about Nicaragua and South Africa and the Tenderloin. Such concern transcended personal betrayals and parental disappointments. It was steady. So there, Gudrun. Well, the silly Swede was ludicrous. What did she have? Some melancholy memories of Nils and a ridiculous attraction to Ernie, of all people. This Gudrun called love? A love better than her own commitments? Love! What do most women have after years as wives and mothers? Widowhood or divorce most likely, and alienated children. Even if your children liked you, what had you accomplished that cows in the field couldn't do? What was the point of reproducing when the world was already overcrowded? What did you win but disappointment in your own conceits? These questions filled Chrissie's chest with a dull vacancy, making her wish for a less rigorous mind. She listened to the soft whish of the rocker against the rug.

'Don't know where she went,' Douglas said to Chrissie half-an-hour later. He inspected the coffee grounds in his big Mummer's mug. 'Somewhere around. Said she needed air. I think she mentioned Woolworth's.'

Chrissie brushed off her apron and thought about 'the Michael telegram'. No reason to think of it, really. Margaret went to Woolworth's all the time. For that glaring shade of lipstick. Or for pizza. Or to soak up the atmosphere. Woolworth's was one of Margaret's quainter habits.

'Chrissie, while there are just the two of us . . .' Douglas cleared his throat.

Chrissie looked about the café, inviting interruption because she hated being the bearer of his harsh confidences.

'That's the last straw with my asshole son.'

Chrissie breathed easier, having heard this song before. 'Runs back to my office this morning and, without so much as a "How are you?", tells me he has to leave town, that he'll be closing the room upstairs for a couple of months.'

Chrissie frowned, remembering her solitude on the rocker, just thirty minutes before. Then she nodded as if she were paying attention.

Douglas waited for her response.

'At least he said goodbye,' she tried.

'Almost the only thing he's said for weeks.'

'And your concerned parental response was?'

Douglas was angry now, his eyes hard. 'I said, "Why are you skipping town two weeks before the election? Afraid your boy is going to get found out?" '

'And?' Chrissie looked more interested now.

'And he says to me, "What do you know about that?" '

She straightened her apron against the stripes of her dress. She would just have to let Douglas talk himself out.

'How my son got mixed up with a crook like Carson!' Douglas was disgusted.

'It's not your fault, if your son, a grown man . . .'

'Especially if he's not my son anymore.'

'What do you mean?'

'I've finally decided to do it. Disown the clown. Started papers this morning. I'm leaving the shop to Roberto. With a provision for Margaret, of course.'

Why was everyone taking care of Miss Margaret? Did they ever leave a 'provision' for Chrissie? Whoever thought of serious, dark, strong Chrissie? A woman of character could take care of herself. Conscious that Douglas was awaiting her reply, she said, 'Don't die yet, man.'

'Sure.' He was impatient. 'I just wanted you to know. You might have to contact the lawyer. I want to be certain that none of my money goes to Kevin's "causes".'

Ernie rushed through the café toward them. 'Margaret,' he looked around. 'Where is Margaret?'

'Probably eating pizza and contemplating street culture.'
Chrissie stopped, noting the horror on Ernie's face.

'Slocum,' he said. 'Someone's shot Slocum!'

'What?' demanded Douglas. 'What!'

Twenty

'Who would kill an old lady's dog?' Roberto ranted. The policeman looked on, blankly. 'What kind of country is this where madmen go around shooting harmless animals? *Madre Mia*!'

They attempted to hold her back. Who were they? Margaret knew Slocum had been trying for home. She reached down to Slocum's warm ears and imagined life draining away. Margaret remembered how peaceful the dog had been that morning, curled beneath the stool, keeping her feet cosy. Now she was dead.

'What is this?' Roger demanded, huffing through the crowd. 'Margaret!' He saw the blood on her dress before she did. 'Margaret, you've been injured. Let me help you.'

'Step back,' the officer called. 'Everybody please move back. This isn't a show.'

'I am a friend of Margaret Sawyer's.' Roger summoned a familiar authority. He was hurt, indignant.

'Yeah, yeah,' said the young cop. 'We're all friends of Margaret's.'

'Sure,' Roberto shouted. 'Even the gangster who murdered her dog. There are lots of friends in the neighborhood. Some better than others.'

So many people. Margaret was dazed. Friends. How could she know so many people?

'All right. All right. Move along.' The policeman took control. 'Take your soap box down the street.'

While the men yelled at each other, Margaret stared at the dead dog, at the blackish red hole ripped through her golden fur. She remembered a stag Bill had brought home once, a beautiful animal except for three bullet wounds in its head. Perfect shots, Bill had said. Perfect. Those open deer eyes had kept her awake for a week. Slocum's eyes, thank God, were closed. Some peace in that. And the blood was a rich, strong color. Blood on the pavement. On her hands. On her dress.

'You, too, Mrs Sawyer.' The policeman had lowered his voice. 'I'm afraid we're going to have to clear up all this. I'll take care of the dog.'

Take care of the dog, she wondered. They wouldn't dump Slocum in the garbage? No. She was too numb to inquire what they would do. Kissing the animal's head, she rose gracefully into the crowd.

Margaret let herself be taken to Mummer's Café. She didn't notice who accompanied her. But she would always remember Chrissie's expression.

Her friend caught the fear immediately and it looked worse on the big-boned Celtic face. Chrissie held alarm and anger in those heavy features. Such a large woman, with a power to her.

Somehow, with Chrissie there, it seemed all right to let go. Margaret stumbled toward her friend in an uncharacteristically awkward movement, hung on Chrissie's broad shoulders, and began to sob. She knew they were all watching — friends, strangers — but she couldn't help it. She just leaned on Chrissie as they walked toward the back of the coffee shop, around by the kitchen where the waitresses took their breaks. She could hear Roberto talking. He had stayed behind, explaining to the shocked customers — a few tourists, but mostly regulars who had known Margaret and Chrissie for years — that someone had shot Slocum. And he, for one, thought it was connected to the race between Marissa Washington and Jake Carson for downtown supervisor.

Nothing quite that coherent ensued at the back table. Margaret hung on Chrissie and wept, 'I don't understand. I don't understand.' Then Roger was speaking. (Yes, Margaret reflected, he must have been the other person who walked her to Mummer's.) Roger was trying to tell Chrissie about Slocum, the blood, the crowd, until Chrissie dissolved him with one of her stares. He leaned back silently, his hands folded, possibly praying.

Twenty-one

They said she was crazy to sit in the news shop like this. They told her to go home and rest. But the apartment would be unbearably large and lonely tonight. She needed company. She needed to see life, even if it was just watching people run from the rain.

Margaret stared out to Geary Street and observed lights fragment a puddle into tiny bright splinters. She glanced up at a child leaning against the telephone pole, throwing rocks into the water. Ten years old at most, with a bored, detached expression. Margaret was often surprised to see children on the block. He was the second boy this week. The other had been younger, a little blond fellow rollerskating in circles around a parking lot on Sunday morning, sleeveless in freezing weather.

Thankfully the fighting had stopped. Chrissie and Roberto and Roger and Ernie and Douglas had all finished their debates and their ministrations. Alone now, she could think about what had really happened.

Slocum was dead? Truly? Or could she reach down now and find her sleeping peacefully, both of them victims and survivors of a bad dream? Slocum shot? She could not believe it. She was not ready for it. How could you be ready for such a thing? Who shoots dogs? Who could have imagined? That's what she had asked herself first. Absurd. Wrong. Ernie must be wrong, she thought when he rushed along the sidewalk shouting. No one shoots dogs, she had wanted to say. What kind of cannibalism? Then she saw poor Slocum gasping on the reddening concrete. She heard the gurgled breathing. Margaret knew she would have to think again. They do shoot dogs. What kind of world was it? She didn't know. Except that it was one where they did shoot dogs.

An accident? She had been staring out the window, past the neon puddles and now she wondered how you could look at something for five minutes without seeing it. What went on in the brain? Why did she see Slocum on the sidewalk now she looked across to Mummer's or down at the apartment buildings? She would ask Ernie. He knew all about nerve cells. And about accidents? Perhaps someone had been practice-shooting and hit poor Slocum. Or perhaps someone had been cleaning his shotgun, like Ernest Hemingway? Or was it vandals? Kids protesting? A mad dog hater? As Margaret avoided the answer, it became clearer. This 'accident' was connected to the election. A warning. A punishment.

That's what she had felt when Michael died. A punishment. She looked at his smiling picture. What had she done to bring such punishment on the boy? Maybe Janey had been right about the evil of that war. But you can't keep a grown man home. She had learned that, in a different way, with Bill. The President had called the war. How could she stop it? Still, for months after Michael's death, she kept herself awake asking how she could have saved him. How could she have raised him differently? Why was it Janey who went to Canada? Why not Michael? It was his life at stake. His life lost. Margaret had tormented herself with these questions until she was so ill they had to hospitalize her. The doctors said she was trying to kill herself, to compensate for his death. But they didn't understand. He wasn't completely dead if you could think about him. He was still alive if she could scrutinize like this. They made her let go. They gave her pills that were stronger than will. Thus Michael died — not in Vietnam, incomprehensible timezones across the Pacific Ocean, but there in her bed at San Francisco Kaiser Hospital.

Just a dog. Margaret stared at the street again. Nothing to compare with the death of a son. Yet it hurt terribly. This death brought back the other in such clear relief. Anyway, Slocum was not just a dog. She was a living creature, a part of life. Oh, how to tell Janey? The girl would have to be told. Maybe this would hasten her visit. No, Margaret didn't want her coming like that, Florence Nightingale, homing to nurse the frail mother. How to tell Janey? She would be devastated. Margaret reminded herself that this was not her fault. She had not shot Slocum.

Kevin's voice. Margaret turned from the window to find the young man leaning against his briefcase against the counter.

146

'Margaret,' he said, as if for the fifth time.

'Yes,' she answered tentatively, unsure of the appropriate language.

'Margaret, I want you to know how sorry I am.'

Willpower. She knew it was taking all his willpower to stay calm. His face was pale. His voice was far away. His eyes were those of the little boy she had known years before. Because the voice was too distant, she concentrated on his lips and all she could see was the dark moustache. Too dark for his hair. It had never seemed natural, that moustache. Child masquerading as Zorro. Or maybe it was a licorice moustache. She often saw licorice when she looked at his lips.

'Don't worry.' Margaret needed to calm Kevin before he tipped her into hysterics. They could talk about the money and the books sometime soon, tomorrow maybe. She would understand better then. Meanwhile, she was absolutely sure he was not involved in this terrible shooting. 'Nothing anyone can do about it now, except feel sad.'

He bit his lower lip, the licorice almost disappearing in the glare of his teeth. The little boy returned. 'I wanted you to know I have to leave town for a while.'

She was taken aback.

'Not for long. Just until . . .' He seemed to change his mind. 'Just until my business is finished.'

What was he asking for? Margaret was too exhausted to understand. 'Goodbye then,' she said, betraying more coolness than she intended.

'Yes.' He looked sad, rather than tense now. 'Bye then.'

Margaret stared again at the neon puddles, pulsing back the life of Geary Street. The neighborhood seemed to be moving very much of its own accord, as it had for the thirty years she had lived here. Why should she disturb it? She could leave that to the young rock throwers. Why should she make trouble for herself? She thought back to September and then ahead to the two weeks left in the campaign and wondered if she could keep her secret from Chrissie.

Good thing it was a slow night at Mummer's. Chrissie had already screwed up three orders. Baked potato instead of french fries. Fruit salad instead of apple pie. And how could

147

she forget that Mrs Dougal liked two dollops of whipped cream in her cocoa? Gudrun had told her to take off sick and relax, but how could she relax when all she wanted was to take care of Margaret, and Margaret was being an old work-horse across the street?

Aye, Chrissie looked out the window, there was Margaret, her back straight, dusting those bloody cigarettes again.

Besides, labor was a purgative for senseless worries. Why did she feel guilty about Slocum's death? It was probably the fault of some hot headed kid trying out his new toy. Or some jealous jackass misfiring (thank God) as he tried to gun down his girlfriend. No, as much as Chrissie considered all the likely possibilities, she couldn't get it out of her head that this shooting had something to do with the election.

Were they trying to slow her down by disabling Margaret? Ernie would laugh at her grandiosity. But Carson's influential friends had already proven that violence was an acceptable campaign tactic in this election. And at this point, ambiguous 'incidents' like this could whittle away morale for Marissa, while an outright attack on her would create a rush of support for the martyr. What would they do next? Try to hit Margaret herself?

Two bells. Mr Poulos's hamburger. Yes, she would make sure it was rare, with pickles on the side. As she delivered the man's supper, she wondered how she could be so civil to her enemies. Poulos was now a big backer of Carson. Out in the open. Legally. Believed in democracy, did Mr Poulos.

'Thanks, Chrissie,' he smiled. 'I'm starving.'

For all his wretched politics, she still liked joking around with Mr Poulos. Such a charmer. Roberto said he was a bastard who paid his clerks under scale until they got the union on his back. Chrissie knew she had to watch her sentimentality, this looking at the good side of people. She had been spending too much time around Margaret.

Suddenly, *he* walked in the door, with all the ease in the world. As though Edinburgh weren't seven thousand miles behind. No, it couldn't be him. But, yes, he looked at Jeanette with the same sweet curiosity. Would there be a place for him here? Two minutes, she heard Jeanette answer. Yes, he nodded patiently. He would wait. Chrissie closed her eyes and told herself to calm down. Breathe. One. Two. Three. Calm down. Rajid was dead. In the street. Blood. Pale doctors spitting out the verdict. Dead on arrival. One less wog. She glanced back to Jeanette, seating him at Gudrun's station.

Chrissie squinted, holding her breath for better focus. No, no, he was too short for Rajid. And lighter. Still, she felt shaken. She did not believe in ghosts. She hardly believed in coincidence. A lot more Indians and Pakistanis were coming to San Francisco as students since it had grown tougher to enter Britain. This was not Rajid. This was no son of Rajid. But she couldn't shake the notion of him. If she hadn't been walking with him, he wouldn't have been their target. She made him visible. She and Rajid might be sitting over at Gudrun's station together if she hadn't . . .

Scrabble. The next night Chrissie and Margaret played until the early morning. Neither of them could sleep. Neither could bear to be apart from the other. Yet they had nothing to talk about.

'Seven letter score,' said Chrissie. 'Come on, hen, you're not going to let me win hands down.'

Margaret pretended to concentrate on her letters.

Chrissie looked around Margaret's apartment and wondered why they always met there. The official reason was that Janey or Rob might phone. Surely the kids could ring back. Truth was, Chrissie considered now, she liked the homeliness of Margaret's studio and she was just as happy to keep her own place to herself.

'I'm sorry.' Margaret's voice was almost inaudible.

'What?' Chrissie spoke loudly, to get her friend's blood running.

'I said I was sorry,' Margaret almost shouted. 'Sometimes you have the sensitivity of a polar bear.'

'Thanks,' said Chrissie, forgetting why she had started this. 'Sorry.'

'Let's not go round again,' declared Chrissie.

'You saw the article?' Margaret asked.

'Yes,' sniffed Chrissie. 'Motive unknown!'

'What do you mean?' Margaret was frightened, 'What do

you know about motives?'

Chrissie searched the familiar face. Something more than grief here. More than fear. Margaret was hiding something.

'Triple word score.' Margaret struck new enthusiasm for the game.

'So what are you holding back?'

'Forty-eight points,' Margaret forced cheerfulness into her voice. '*You*'re the one who's holding back. Make sure you add that to *my* column.'

Maybe she was imagining things, reconsidered Chrissie. Maybe she was so desperate for a resolution, an absolution, that she was imagining things.

She looked over to see Margaret's foot reaching across the rug for Slocum. Margaret caught Chrissie's glance and rubbed her ankle against the coffee table, pretending to scratch.

Their eyes met once more. Neither woman was prepared for the anguish. Margaret struggled unsuccessfully to hold back tears. They streamed down her face, eroding gulleys through the powder and rouge.

'Can't help it.' She stopped and started, choking in the wetness as though she were swimming upstream, gasping for breath. 'I just don't understand. What did I do? Poor dog. I just don't understand.'

Chrissie moved over to the couch and hugged her weeping friend.

'Why?' Margaret returned. 'Why? Why?'

'I don't know, love.' Saying this aloud frightened Chrissie so that she too began softly to cry.

Twenty-two

They were talking as if Margaret weren't there. They had done this for the last two days. Not that she had ever been a chatterbox, but lately she was mute. She also couldn't eat. Couldn't let anything in or out. She felt as if her mind and body were in different worlds.

At first they had been solicitous, bringing her sandwiches and cups of hot soup. Ernie auditioned a new comedy routine. Roger phoned hourly. Douglas offered her time off to go to the Flower Show. After several days they gave up. Life continued around her as if she were in a coma, alert only to the exchange of coins and newspapers. So this morning Douglas, Charles and Ernie stood in a knot, arguing about the 'incident' as if she weren't there.

'What's wrong with your buddies on the force?' Douglas asked. 'After all, the dog was killed in broad daylight. Are there that many madmen shooting animals that you couldn't find one suspect?'

Charles was silent, his eyes toughening from defense to resistance.

'Give him a break,' said Ernie. 'His supervisors won't permit any more time.'

'You mean Carson has purchased the entire police force?' Douglas paused to fill his pipe. 'Development must be very profitable indeed. Eleven days till the election. Everything's closing in.'

'How are you so sure it's connected to the election?' said Ernie. 'Doesn't make any sense to me. Why a dog? Why Margaret's dog?'

Margaret sat straighter, crossing and uncrossing her legs over the endless space between the stool and the floor. She reminded herself again that silence was the best tactic. If Slocum's death were connected to the books and the money, her silence would prove she had got their message. 'They.'

151

Who were 'they'? She still had a hard time believing that Kevin was involved in Carson's bigotry and violence. Surely the boy had nothing to do with Slocum's death.

'Law and order,' drawled Douglas. 'Needed some random assault to support his platform. He keeps talking about how dangerous this neighborhood is. So he picks a dog. His thugs might threaten Marissa, but they'd never touch her, that would just bring a rush of sympathy against him. But killing a dog will get people riled up about law and order.'

Margaret sat back against the stool.

Ernie and Charles shrugged.

Finally, Charles answered, 'Lots of crazy people in the city. Anyone could have done it. I've talked to everyone on this block twice. Nobody saw a thing.'

'Memory comes cheap in a depression,' Douglas concluded.

'Well, if he's buying memories as well as votes,' said Ernie, 'where do you think he's getting all the money?'

'The World Bank,' Douglas puffed. 'The Rockefellers.'

The Rockefellers, Margaret thought wistfully. It seemed years since she and Roberto had joked about that trip to Mexico.

'So where's Kevin?' asked Ernie.

'Don't know.' Douglas was terse.

Ernie registered his concern and Margaret stared at him, hoping to disconnect the next thought. Instead, Ernie caught her eye and asked, 'Do *you* know, Margaret?'

'He said he had to leave town for a few weeks — on business.'

Ernie and Charles frowned.

'And I'm trying not to imagine what kind of business.' declared Douglas. 'It's too much. One thing to sire a good-for-nothing. But a common criminal!'

'Stop it,' burst Margaret. 'Just stop it right now! Stop suspecting and maligning someone who isn't here to defend himself. Stop this incessant talk about poor Slocum. Stop all this arguing about the election and Carson and the developers. Politics. Politics. Politics. Is that all you think about? Can't you see I need a little peace?' She finished, surprised at her outburst and further surprised that she didn't regret a word of it.

'How about a coffee, Margaret?' Charles broke the silence.

'Thank you, Charles. I think I'll just take it on my own,'

she looked down at her watch, 'since it's time for lunch. Good day, Douglas.'

'Farewell, Margaret.' Douglas tamped his pipe assiduously as if he might find indifference mingled with the tobacco. '*Bon appétit.*'

Outside the air smelled fresher than it had for months. The delicate atmosphere after the heavy storm showed no hint of rain. Margaret set out for Union Square. Crossing Mason Street, she heard her name being called by someone coming down the hill.

Roger, of course. Disappointment settled. She had completely forgotten their lunch date. A minute more, she thought shamefully, and she would be out of sight. However she was caught now. Turning toward him, she tried to mask her fatigue. 'Roger! Hello there.'

'How nice of you to meet me halfway,' he declared.

She noticed the pink in his cheeks, his determined health, and wondered at the depth of her sudden hostility toward him.

'Mannings,' he repeated louder, over the street noise. 'Didn't you suggest Manning's yesterday?'

'Yes,' she shouted above the drilling machines, honking horn, rattling exhaust pipes, groaning bus.

'So how are you?' Roger called and abruptly the drilling stopped, stripping the street to relative silence. They both looked down, embarrassed by their exposed voices. 'Are you feeling any better?'

'Yes,' she nodded.

He offered his arm, but she pretended not to notice.

Once inside the cafeteria, she lost her appetite. She regarded the prepared food hardening under bright warming lights. Janey had said these dishes reminded her of specimens in a biology lab and Margaret had never been able to loosen that image from her mind. Such food seemed an act of obscenity, three dimensional graffiti about 'the downtown community'.

'The macaroni looks delicious,' Roger enthused.

Margaret was confounded how this habitué of French restaurants could select that sticky thick mess for his tray. Who did he think he was humoring, a starving body from Red China? Margaret stopped herself. Really, why was she so angry with Roger?

'I think I'll have the onion soup.' The clear, hot substance looked the least toxic choice.

Roger patted her shoulder. She tried not to recall the way he patted Slocum, a man fastidiously tolerant of innocent animals.

They sat silently for a few minutes. Margaret glanced at the dishevelled woman dozing into her newspaper. In a booth by the wall, a palsied old man talked to himself. And behind him sat a rather prim mother and daughter, probably visiting the city for a shopping expedition. Manning's was a funny place, one of those border stations between Tenderloin dwellers and tourists from San Rafael. The cafeteria didn't have a bathroom of its own. You had to go next door to the Stewart Hotel and pay ten cents. Margaret thought pay toilets were against the law and if they weren't, they certainly should be.

Finally, Roger spoke. 'You're still terribly sad, my dear.'

Margaret nodded with tears in her eyes, grateful that he talked emotions instead of politics.

'I wish there were some comfort.' He reached over for her hand. She forced herself to let him take it. 'I wish I could offer some wise words.'

'You've been very kind.' she said.

'I love you Margaret,' he explained.

This was just what she didn't want to hear because even as he spoke she knew she could not love him. She had tried. She thought of the man on the hotel roof. She remembered the stirring noon lectures. He was a compassionate, intelligent man. What could she say?

'You've been very kind,' she repeated and lifted a spoon of warm soup to her lips.

Twenty-three

REMEMBER THE DOG. STOP MEDDLING.

The first threat arrived in Chrissie's mailbox. White business envelope. No return address. San Francisco postmark of the previous day. Lined yellow paper with magazine letters pasted in a row. Chrissie stood in the lobby, her mouth as wide open as the mailbox. A meticulous job, she noted, wondering what kind of spirit lent itself to such sinister behavior. Completely untraceable, just like you saw in the movies. Too melodramatic to be genuine? No, she feared this was quite real.

Chrissie shut the mailbox and calmly proceeded upstairs. She made some tea and collapsed in her chair. REMEMBER THE DOG. STOP MEDDLING. What did they know about her? She rocked back and forth. And how did they know what she knew about them? Back and forth. What *did* she know? More than she thought she knew, that's certain, because so far it was nothing worth being shot for.

Back and forth. She was simply observing Carson's campaign expenses. Just a little snooping. Visiting the Registrar of Voters. Any fool could see Carson was spending more than he claimed. Still, the others in Marissa's campaign insisted on fighting ideology. Of course she, also, would prefer to see Carson defeated on issues at the polls rather than on deportment in the newspapers.

Chrissie got up from the rocker and paced the living-room. Certainly she would rather see voters say 'no' to development and 'yes' to local control. So she kept canvassing for Marissa. But since Slocum was shot, she was certain Marissa would need more than canvassing. And the election was a week Tuesday.

Chrissie looked out the window. Across the street, by the fire hydrant, she could see Douglas chatting to Ernie. No trace of nasty September smog. October was a colder, clearer month. Roberto wheeled a big stack of papers. Reassured for some reason, she returned to her chair and poured another cup of tea.

The second letter came two days later and scared her more. Under the apartment door. It wasn't hard to enter the building. Still, she had frozen at the sight of the envelope. She opened the letter before the door itself. How did she know they weren't inside with a machine gun? No, it wouldn't come to that, she convinced herself. Too messy. Too obvious. More likely a hit and run, counting on the slowness of her old legs. Or poison in the tea. She wondered if it were someone at Mummer's. LAST WARNING, SNOOPER, the letter said. 'Seedy business,' Chrissie scoffed at the fear burning in her stomach. A cup of tea would help. She dropped the second letter on the coffee table next to Marissa's campaign brochures. As she fussed in the kitchen, Chrissie thought back to the previous day's conversation with gratitude and chagrin.

'You gotta watch out for these public accusations, honey.' Marissa intently stirred the sugar into her coffee. She subsisted on coffee. Might have injected it if the needlemarks wouldn't cause a scandal.

'And I suppose I should regard you as a shining example of public restraint?' Chrissie grinned.

'They expect me to behave that way.' Marissa was used to volleying with her friend.

'That's why they've threatened your life?' Chrissie did not mention her own warning letter. She did not want to burden Marissa. Did not want Marissa to pull her from the campaign. Momentarily, it occurred to Chrissie that she was always protecting people, even if it was just protecting them from truth about herself.

'They're not going to do anything as long as I keep it in the open.' Marissa held Chrissie's arm. 'It's in their interest to provide me with a bodyguard. I know that now. I'm not worried like I was in the beginning.'

Chrissie peered through Marissa's bravado, to the terror and courage which drove her and generated the whole campaign.

Marissa shrugged, gulped the rest of her coffee and stood.

'I've never been able to tell you a thing.' She shook her head. 'Don't know why that should change now. Just be careful, honey. There will be other elections; there's only one Chrissie.'

'They broke the mold.' Chrissie tried to conceal her pleasure at Marissa's fondness. The other woman bent down and kissed her on the forehead, drawing a bright blush across Chrissie's cheeks.

'Take care,' Chrissie said. She loathed this expression that even telephone operators said nowadays, but it dispelled her selfconsciousness.

'See you at the White House,' waved Marissa. 'The day we paint it.' She picked up the bill, rushing off to her next appointment.

Chrissie pushed the ugly letter aside as she set down the tea pot. Restlessly she surveyed the campaign literature on her coffee table. Drawn to the brochure with Marissa's proud smile on the cover, she thought about what an exceptional person Marissa was. A fine friend.

Occasionally, Chrissie worried whether she'd lose Marissa altogether once she became supervisor. She would be so busy then, making contacts with city officials, attending meetings. Well, it just didn't bear thinking about, did it? You couldn't let personal things like that interfere with commitment.

She stacked the campaign flyers and collected the two wretched letters, tucking them beneath her Rock of Edinburgh paperweight. That was the best thing to do with these threats, dismiss them for the moment. Nothing more than the work of cowardice. People who threatened didn't kill.

Sun streaked low across the room, over Chrissie's shoulder, catching James's picture and the silver on her dresser. It must have escaped from behind the grey for a moment. She turned to calculate the space between clouds, to determine how long the warmth might last. Swivelling back, her glance was caught by the shining silver brush and comb. Rajid had saved an entire year to purchase that from Jensen's window. An entire year at the brewery, packing brown bottles into wooden crates. A year of splinters in his hands and cracks in his face from the uncivilized cold. For this he had left the warmth of India? No, for college, he reminded her. When he got his degree they could go anywhere they wanted, to London or Paris or Rome. His science degree would be an unrestricted passport. London. Paris. Rome. A year of saving shillings in between tuition and board and weekly cinema. A year of saving and then he took their plans with him into the ground.

Chrissie remembered how the ground was almost too cold to dig. It was with great sympathy and a certain relief that her brothers supported her through the funeral. She would have to stop crying. It was over. She would recover. It was sad, they comforted her, but it was over. She could not tell them about the threatening glances she got from men as she walked home late at night. Were they the murderers? Too dark to tell. It would always be too dark to tell. Wog whore, someone shouted two weeks after they had buried Rajid. She turned around to the voice and chased nothing into the distance, all the way to Wellington's statue. Were they threatening her? Was she frightened of them? Had she left Scotland because she was afraid? Or because it would always be too dark to tell and too cold to feel?

She picked up the tea cup, more to heat her hands than to drink from it. She would not run away from these melo-dramatic threats. Marissa was right about remaining too visible for danger. Chrissie would just stay as visible as a gadfly — as elusive as a firefly — and what harm could come to her?

They wouldn't want murder on their hands. Once you analyzed it calmly, that was obvious. Oh, maybe a dog. Clever to get at Chrissie through Margaret. They could be that despicable. But anything more would be madness.

Odd, how Margaret had got mixed up in this. You could think it was Margaret running for office, the way all the activity swarmed around her. Everyone came to Margaret — Kevin and Douglas; Roger the Reverend and Gudrun the whore; Mrs Dougal and Roberto. What was it about Margaret that drew them? Her 'openness', Ernie would say. All very well. However Chrissie always said that kind of openness could be dangerous.

Twenty-four

Gradually Margaret felt better. She knew she would recover; if she survived, she would recover. Writing to Janey had helped. And the passing of time, seven days gone. Now only a week left until that damned election. She thought less about Slocum. She was not so terrified. She tried to accept that it was an accident, or at least an 'incident' as the paper described it. POLICE CLOSE INVESTIGATION OF DOG INCIDENT. At first, she was surprised the papers covered the story, but as Douglas predicted, they reported it as symptomatic of violence escalating in the Tenderloin. Margaret wished Chrissie would calm down. On Saturday she had questioned people all over the street. Still she was quizzing everyone who walked into Mummer's. Chrissie would lose her job if she didn't stop this nonsense. If she didn't lose it for all the sick leave she was taking to work on Marissa's campaign.

'Morning, Margaret.' Roger. Cheerful as always. Incorrigibly positive. Last night he was sorry she hadn't been able to see him. Yet he had understood. Dear Roger. Ineffectual Roger. How could she tell him they were destined for fond friendship? She was sure of this now, sure that life would be too, well, bland with him. He would provide the security and she would create the momentum. He was a good man, but she was too old to be tied down. How did she know so suddenly? Slocum's death had put her own life in sharp relief. But the real question about her feelings for Roger was why did it take her so long to figure them out?

'Morning, Roger. Fine day.'

'You're feeling better?' he inquired.

'Yes, thanks.'

'So how about lunch? A little nutrition goes a long way.'

'I can't,' she lied. 'I have a plan with Gudrun. Maybe later in the week?'

'Margaret,' he stiffened. 'Is there something I should know?'

Perhaps he was trying to make the break easier for her. She regarded him with tentative gratitude.

'About Slocum?' he asked. 'Or Janey? Is there something you want to share?'

'No,' she said carefully. 'I don't think so.' What a mess. Why was she knotted by all these unspoken words? She felt responsible for explaining that this affair would not work just as she felt responsible for revealing the bribes. Kevin had left town. It wasn't happening any more. She couldn't change the past. Why did it all fall on her as she sat in the shop minding her own business? She hadn't asked for romance, fraud and violence.

'All right,' Roger's tone was businesslike. He picked up a *Chronicle*, apparently forgetting that she knew he had a home subscription. 'I guess I'll see you later in the week.'

Margaret waved goodbye. She knew he would not put up a struggle and she felt a touch of resentment. Because he didn't push, the entire weight fell on her. Just once she wished he would show his forcefulness, some voice of his own. This left her feeling ashamed. But what had she done? She would just go home and rest, just lie down and let the hours pass over her and perhaps somewhere she would find sleep.

Douglas approached the cash register in silence, as if her muteness were contagious. They exchanged accounts quickly. Within minutes, Margaret was standing in the elevator rising to her apartment.

'Psychic energy,' Gudrun called it when unrelated events converged. Margaret was too worried about the bribery and too distraught about Slocum. Of course they had nothing to do with each other. She had just imagined that.

As Margaret walked down the corridor, she felt an edge of hunger. Good sign. She would break into that sharp cheddar that Chrissie had brought last night. Cheese and one of those Granny Smith apples and an English muffin. That would be enough to fill her. Maybe enough to make her a little sleepy.

She noticed an envelope sticking under the door. Shaking, she inserted her key in the lock. Why was she shaking? Because none of her friends left messages this way. She chained the door securely behind her. Then she picked up the envelope.

Calmly, Margaret made herself sit down on the couch before opening the envelope. She ripped it, anyway, taking off a tip of the letter. Yellow paper. Unfolding the lined sheet, she saw words taped from a magazine. All different sizes and colors. CALL OFF THE HOUNDS. NOSEY FRIENDS CAN GET HURT.

Margaret imagined herself in a large, white room, sun patching the blank walls. She was alone in a silent, sterilized chamber and she felt strangely relieved. This settled it. She would have to tell Chrissie. Then came the old fear, nipping like a pinched nerve. How much would she have to tell her? How much could she still protect . . . protect whom?

Chrissie walked briskly, arguing with herself about Slocum. She never believed the murderer was a 'misfiring miscreant' as Ernie put it. When she told him she thought the dog's death had something to do with the election, Ernie said she had a one-track mind. Single tracks lead somewhere, she answered. At least she was doing something. Chrissie was moving down Geary Street, toward Larkin, in search of Gudrun's friend who said he had a lead.

Outside the Bank of America, near Jones, she noticed a red-faced man jerkily stuffing two twenty dollar bills into his wallet. She wanted to shake him for his recklessness, to take him to the Salvation Army detox center on Turk, to shout some warning to him. Instead she strode more quickly, her right thumb playing against the arthritic twinge slithering up her left wrist.

'Not so fast, Sherlock Holmes.'

Douglas's voice. Yes, Douglas. She shouldn't be surprised. She tried never to be surprised on the street. She always watched closely, tuned to any kind of change. It could be a car coming on the sidewalk. A person walking out of the shadows to serenade you. Kids running, in some innocent-dangerous game. Music from a panhandling trumpeteer who's just found extra wind. A purse snatcher. A mad sniper. An old friend.

'Hello, Douglas.' Chrissie was brusque, partly because she was in a hurry and partly because Douglas had been singularly unhelpful lately.

'Where are you going now? Following another lead?'

'As a matter of fact.' Chrissie noticed how she sounded more Scottish when she was angry.

'Don't you think this sort of thing could get you in trouble.' His voice softened and his face was worried.

'Walking down the street in broad daylight? asking questions of fellow citizens?'

'Chrissie.' Douglas was exasperated.

'Tell me what you mean,' she demanded. 'What should I be afraid of?'

'Of being shot.'

'Aye, I am scared of rocks through windows. And explosions. Being shot is only one more liability.'

'Chrissie, this is different.' He held his trenchcoat tightly around him. 'You don't go out looking for people to plant bombs.'

'Are you sure it's me you're worried about?' she asked.

'What do you mean?'

'I mean Kevin. Are you afraid that I'll find out something about him?'

Douglas rooted around his pocket for his pipe and stared over Chrissie's ample shoulder, watching a Muni bus wheeze to the curb.

'Tell me truthfully, Douglas, don't you have a terrible feeling about Kevin.'

He concentrated on the pipe, on depositing a precise amount of tobacco in the bowl, on nesting it correctly. He struck the match on the side of his shoe and squinted at the flame, sucking smoke between them.

Finally, he met her steady eyes. 'Yes, I am worried. Stupid guy.'

'It's gone beyond that,' she said carefully. 'This violence is insanity.'

He waited.

'And I want to make sure it doesn't get worse.' Chrissie ignored the futility in her own voice.

'Let me know what you find out.' He concentrated on the spiral of sweet smoke. 'And be careful.'

Chrissie continued down the street feeling more alone than she had felt in years. She considered how violence isolated people, sending them to private defenses. Gudrun tried to ignore the whole thing. Sad the dog is dead, she said, but there were more urgent *human* problems to ponder. Ernie expressed concern for Margaret and then avoided the topic. Back to the election. Back to his flirtation with Charles. Back to the Bette Davis Revival at the Castro Theatre. Douglas was frightened in a different way, close-mouthed because of Kevin, hoping silence would protect his son, would camouflage 'the incident'. Bentman, of course, saw it as a cross to bear, as a fact of life to accept with faith. His happy talk was driving Chrissie mad and, she noticed, was beginning to wear thin on Margaret.

Chrissie's heel caught behind her. Gum on the sidewalk. Damn. She scraped it off and looked down. More gum. Cigarette butts. Spit. Pieces of paper. Up the street, she saw steam rising from a manhole, as if from a cauldron. She calmed herself. Don't lose control. You have to look wise on the street. It's too tempting to observe or gawk rather than watch. Safety is an expression in your eyes. By the way you watch you are visible or invisible, inviting back a glance, an attack. Safety is a certain way of standing. It has nothing to do with how old or frail or thin or feminine you look. It has all to do with determination and awareness. The best protection is in the eyes, always to be looking around.

Margaret was the most unpredictable. Chrissie returned to her inventory as she continued up Geary Street. Some days Margaret walked as if blindfolded, unsure of the length of the pavement and the height of steps. Some evenings she would rage with tears. The reactions were so extreme. Chrissie desperately wished she could help Margaret reassemble her world. She would settle for less, for just being able to communicate with Margaret again. Her friend had faded like an overexposed photo. Douglas was wrong. She wasn't looking for trouble; she was looking for Margaret.

FALSE ALARM IN CARSON CAMPAIGN. Margaret read the afternoon article with mixed emotions. 'Allegations of illegal contributions to the Carson campaign were dropped this morning when . . .'

Maybe it would stop now. Maybe they would see she wasn't

163

going to the police. Maybe now Chrissie would be out of danger. Maybe she wouldn't even have to mention that horrible letter. No, of course she would have to tell her. Still, why would Chrissie suspect Kevin? She didn't know anything about his money.

She looked forward to seeing Chrissie with dread and relief. For the last few hours since the threatening letter, she had felt dazed, worse than she had felt at Slocum's death. Frantically, she tried to phone Chrissie at home, at Mummer's, at headquarters. Unable to reach her, she couldn't bring herself to talk to anyone else. She had just reviewed the troubles over and over in her mind. How had she got caught up in politics? She always knew electioneering brought trouble. She felt an old place in her stomach, a childhood place, which ached with a vague sense of guilt and confusion. What had she done? This was like when Mom and Pop died. Sadness was understandable, but where did she get this unallaying fear that she had caused their deaths? Later she had heard that all orphans reacted that way. Still, the fear continued to haunt her in different shapes.

'Nice day.' Roberto held the door open with his foot as he shifted newspapers from the sidewalk into the shop. 'Have the Rockefellers dropped any money in your lap lately?'

Margaret looked up, alarmed. 'Money, what money?'

Startled by the strain on Margaret's face, Roberto lowered his voice. 'I think you need a holiday more than ever from this place. When are you and Chrissie going to Hawaii?'

'After the . . .' she sat straighter, 'election.' The color rose in her cheeks as she recognized his reference to the Rockefellers.

'Douglas around?'

'Ill today.'

'The bull sick?' Roberto's eyes widened. 'What's wrong?'

'Don't know,' said Margaret. 'He phoned an hour ago and said he had the 'flu.'

'Family troubles?'

'Sorry?' shrugged Margaret, irritated by her own distraction.

'Douglas,' mused Roberto. 'Do you think this is the Kevin influenza?'

'Could be.'

164

'Discreet,' said Roberto. 'Isn't that what Chrissie called you? And what was it you called her? "Meddlesome." Yes, that was it.'

Margaret winced, realizing how loud their argument had been. Horrible that Roberto had memorized the whole exchange!

'Maybe you're right.' He spoke absently. 'I'm not sure that all this personal stuff matters at a time when we're about to lose the neighborhood.'

Margaret sighed.

'You read the headlines?' He shook his head bitterly. 'But you probably don't know the worst. Seven days to go and Marissa's broke. This last week of the campaign, when we should be doing a big publicity push, she's hardly got a cent.'

Margaret started to weep.

'Mama, *que pasa?*'

'Nothing,' Margaret sniffed. 'Just the stress. I don't understand what I . . . I don't understand how I . . .' She caught herself, so out of control, her mind wandering. She really must do something. She must talk with Chrissie. What should she say? How much should she say?

Distressed, Roberto asked, 'Have you talked to Chrissie?'

'Chrissie,' Margaret responded slowly. 'What do you mean, Chrissie?'

'Chrissie.' Roberto adopted his teasing voice. 'Your *hermana*, Chrissie. The lass with the knobbly knees who owns the gourmet restaurant across the street.'

Margaret searched Roberto's dark eyes and remembered the Rockefellers.

Talk to Chrissie, she said calmly to herself. And then to Roberto, 'Talk to Chrissie, yes, I'll do that right away.'

Twenty-five

Margaret could hardly believe they were on the bus together, safely leaving the war zone. She stared out of the window, recalling how frantically she had tried to reach Chrissie last night. When Chrissie finally answered the phone at 6 am, she gruffly explained that she had taken a sick leave from Mummer's to do some 'campaign work'. Margaret didn't remember what she had said; maybe it was just her tone of voice that persuaded Chrissie to extend her sick leave and go to Golden Gate Park with her today.

Might as well be on separate buses, thought Chrissie, her long face expressing how much she did not want to be going to the Japanese Tea Garden. She had better things to do six days before the election. Besides, she had never liked how the Tea Garden bound their waitresses in those tight kimonos.

Her memory throbbed from the last visit, when they had talked about Bentman, avoided talking about him, then talked about him again. Maybe that was Margaret's mission today. Oh, crikey, she was going to marry the ass and wanted her to be maid of honor! Calm down. Chrissie inhaled sharply. Why imagine the worst? Probably Margaret just needed a rest from the neighborhood. That's why Douglas had given her the day off. She was still pretty distraught from Slocum's death.

Margaret continued staring out of the window, searching for something to say, something to pass the time. She felt as if she were using up all her energy moving the streetcar to the park. She had tried a couple of topics — Janey's visit, Douglas's recovery from the flu — but Chrissie seemed uninterested. So she went back to powering the streetcar. It was a fine, late Indian summer afternoon and she forced herself to notice the sun brightening hills of pastel houses.

Golden Gate Park was surprisingly crowded for a weekday, observed Margaret, as if half the workers of San Francisco had called in sick. She appreciated the crowds. Distraction made the silence between herself and Chrissie less awkward. She watched, amazed, as a bald man danced on rollerskates to some lively music from his earphones. Skateboards, bicycles, rollerskates. Didn't they teach people to walk anymore?

'Wheels.' Chrissie read her mind. 'Wheels and digital clocks and pocket calculators. It's as if a certain sort of intelligence had landed on the planet.'

In silence again they made their way through the bonsai trees to the Tea Garden.

A young waitress waddled forward with menus. Chrissie waved them away, ordering the special.

Cookies. Margaret imagined the sweet, hard lumps and wondered how she could swallow anything that afternoon. Maybe this was the wrong place to talk with Chrissie after all. Someone might overhear. Maybe she should wait until they were home. She might get Ernie to join them. Now they could just talk about Hawaii.

Chrissie knew the direct approach never worked with Margaret. Whatever was bothering her would come out in its own time. Margaret called *her* a stubborn mule, but Margaret was much tougher. The woman could have taught passive resistance to Ghandi.

Soon the silence grew stifling to Chrissie. 'I can't believe Marissa. Such a trooper. Managed to get that loan to finish the campaign. I think she keeps her eyes open with toothpicks. Whether she gets elected or not we should send her to the hospital when it's all over.'

Margaret nodded. Regardless of what she thought about politics, she had always admired Marissa. Admired the kind of strength that Chrissie was describing, but also liked her positive nature. Marissa believed conditions would improve. If only she could borrow some of that optimism. While she fished for a way to express this praise, the waitress arrived.

Crack. Margaret opened her fortune cookie even before Chrissie poured the tea. She looked up in embarrassment, but her friend hadn't noticed. Chrissie was swishing around the tea, mesmerized by the pot, as if it were a crystal ball.

Margaret extended her cup. She relished the warmth filling her hands from the small, round bowl. She loved drinking tea this way. At home she had taken to pouring it into glasses, so she might enjoy the warmth before she sipped.

'Margaret.' Chrissie was exasperated. She reminded herself to be gentle, to prod, but carefully. 'Margaret, hen, is there something on your mind?'

'Oh, no, I just wanted . . .' Margaret paused at Chrissie's frown. She thought of her friend's reluctance to come to the Tea Garden. She looked down at the cookie, then pulled it apart. Unfolding the narrow white slip, she knew her deliberateness must be maddening to Chrissie, but she couldn't help it. She needed something to concentrate on, ' "Prosperity will come soon," ' she read and then did not know whether to laugh or cry.

'Used fortunes,' Chrissie complained. 'Used fortunes . . .' She noticed Margaret's lowered head, the tears seeping between her fingers into the small plate with the cracked cookie.

'Margaret,' she spoke softly.

Margaret could not answer. She was far away, in a pain as deep as all the unfairness of her life. She tried to talk, but slipped back into the confusion. Why? Why me? How did I? Fury, fear and a heavy sadness contained her.

'Margaret.' Chrissie gripped her friend's shoulder.

Margaret opened her fingers and regarded the familiar blue eyes which she trusted more than her own. Still, she could not talk.

'It's all right, Margaret.' Chrissie felt settled by the physical contact. 'Take your time, love.'

'Chris —' but Margaret could not finish the word without a choke and a heavy sob. She drew apart and fumbled in her purse.

Chrissie, mistaking the gesture, handed her a handkerchief.

Margaret brushed it away and pulled out the lined yellow sheet she had found beneath her door.

Chrissie stared, a brief pitch of alarm emitting from her throat. Her jaw tightened. 'My God,' she said. Angrily she flipped over the paper for identifying marks. Finally she returned to Margaret, whose face was still flattened by fear.

'Oh, Margaret, love, I'm sorry. How did you get mixed up in all this?'

Margaret felt the terror loosen. For a moment, she thought

Chrissie might tell her it had been an hallucination. Then she recognized that what had scared her most was Chrissie's judgment.

'Tell me everything,' said Chrissie.

Late that afternoon they returned to Geary Street where Margaret insisted on preparing supper.

Chrissie's eyebrows were rigid.

'Yes?' said Margaret.

'It's a good story, hen, but how are we going to get people to believe it?'

'What do you mean, "story"?' demanded Margaret. 'What do you mean, "get people to believe it"? You act as if I imagined it all.'

'Hang about,' said Chrissie. '*I* believe you.' She paused, chasing a chunk of tunafish across her plate. She had never got used to these 'casseroles' as Margaret called them. She knew she shouldn't feel insulted, Margaret fed this slop to her own children. However Chrissie had always eaten heartily rather than delicately. She wanted to feel full from a dinner — warmed by the food, sedated by the wine, awakened by the coffee. She had simple, clear expectations of eating which had nothing to do with herbs and garlic. Chrissie was a meat and potatoes woman, even if it were minced beef and chips. She liked to see what she was eating. Her stomach behaved better, being prepared by her eyes for what was to follow down the gullet.

She looked back to Margaret. 'It's just that newspapers are so petrified of libel that they whitewash the issues. You can't make allegations about a candidate a few days before the election without some fairly stiff proof.'

Margaret was, as always, impressed with Chrissie's sophistication about situations and strategies. She was also baffled. 'So?'

'So,' Chrissie closed her eyes for patience, 'how are we going to find the charming red-haired chap who was making these missions of mercy for Kevin? Advertise in the classifieds?'

'But I told you, I saw him on TV. He's one of Carsons aides.'

'Sure, sure. So where's our proof about the books? Who will corroborate your testimony?'

Margaret thought Chrissie got a little self-important with the language she borrowed from Perry Mason. No matter, her friend was right. Only one other person could testify that she had passed money in the books.

'Smuggling cash that way was risky,' Chrissie continued, 'also very clever. If you press charges, it'll be Carson's word against that of an old woman.'

Would Chrissie ever stop this old woman business?

'Kevin,' Margaret spoke, as if recalling a mantra. 'We'll just have to find Kevin.'

Startled by her — naïvety? determination? — Chrissie slowly agreed, 'Aye, we will have to find Kevin.'

Douglas didn't want to hear anything about it.

After closing, he sat with Chrissie and Margaret in the back of his shop, the front section darkened against persistent trick-or-treaters. 'More brandy?' He handed the bottle to Chrissie, who had taken her first glass in two gulps.

'Thank you.' She watched him carefully. Was he trying to get her loaded so she would stop tormenting him? She glanced over at Margaret's hand, steady under a still full glass.

Douglas repeated abruptly, 'I don't want to hear anything about it. He's no son of mine.'

'Not true,' Chrissie spoke up. 'It's precisely because he is a son of yours that you don't want to know.'

'Of course,' Margaret said quietly. She couldn't believe Chrissie's bullheadedness. Of course he wouldn't want to send his son to jail. It was one thing to scold Kevin and quite another to incriminate him.

Douglas and Chrissie turned to her.

'That makes perfect sense.' Margaret was remorseful. 'We're putting you in an impossible position, Douglas, and I'm sorry.' She put down her glass, then gathered her purse and coat.

He sighed. 'I don't know where the boy is. I guess I've never known where he was. Anyway, I can't help you. I don't want anything more to do with him.'

Chrissie shook her head in disgust. They thought she didn't understand because she wasn't a parent. Maybe they were right. She hadn't reproduced a being who was more important to her than her principles. What was so holy about family, she would never know.

'Believe me,' Douglas said to Chrissie. 'I can't help you.'

Margaret watched Chrissie advance toward the shop the next morning and wondered why she wasn't worrying more. Chrissie seemed to have taken charge of everything, including her fear. Besides, since the Tea Garden, the scenes had been shifting too swiftly for Margaret to feel much of anything.

'Spencer has agreed to run an item in his "Newsnose" column,' Chrissie whispered to Margaret although there was no one else in the shop.

'Who reads that silly underground thing?' Margaret was surprised at her own belligerence. At least it was something. What had *she* done?

'Alternative medium,' smiled Chrissie. 'A lot of people read it. *A lot more* after this article appears. Wait till you see what I've said.'

'You didn't let them use your name?' Margaret was flabbergasted.

'Well, he could hardly run something like that without attribution. He's not so worried about getting sued. He doesn't have much money to lose. But he's got to stay credible.'

'Chrissie, don't you take these threats seriously?' Margaret's throat tightened. 'If you don't, I do. Here.' She handed Chrissie the phone. 'Call him now and take it out. You heard me.'

'Too late.' Chrissie's lilt was exaggerated slightly to keep her above panic. 'It should come out this afternoon.'

'You've got to be kidding.' Roberto rushed in the door. 'How come you never told us about any of this?'

'A scoop is a scoop.' Chrissie was impressed by the calm in her own voice.

'What does it say?' Margaret asked nervously. 'What about Chrissie. What about me?'

'You?' asked Roberto. '*Claro*! Now I put it together.' He handed Margaret the pink tabloid newspaper. 'It doesn't say a word about *you*, Mama.'

Margaret read aloud:

FIVE DAZE BEFORE THE ELECTION

> What small-time developer has been
> smuggling money to what downtown
> supervisorial candidate whose name
> rhymes with arson?

Chrissie chuckled. Margaret continued:

> The question of the week comes from
> sprightly senior activist Chrissie MacInnes.

Margaret peered over the top of the paper.

Chrissie was still wincing at the word, 'sprightly.'

When Margaret caught her friend's eye, she inquired, 'Protecting everyone but yourself?'

Chrissie shrugged.

'That bastard Kevin,' Roberto shook his head.

'How do you know?' Margaret was astonished.

Chrissie grinned. 'You ought to go into newspapers.'

'I am "in newspapers",' he barked, 'just the quiet end of the business. Like Mama here.'

'Quiet!' Margaret shuddered.

'But the question,' Roberto spoke as if he were also a veteran Perry Mason fan, 'is how to get Kevin to admit that —' He interrupted himself, 'The question is how to find Kevin. Slime. Such slime.'

'Confused boy,' Margaret contradicted him irritably. 'You know what it's like for kids with no mother. At least your girls have their Aunt Rosa. Kevin had no one.'

'Except you,' said Chrissie.

'And Mrs Hartley,' Margaret recalled.

'The one he was sending all those mysteries to?' Chrissie began to laugh, then grew serious. 'There really is a Mrs Hartley?'

Margaret was taken aback by her urgency. 'I think so. There used to be.'

Roberto and Chrissie exchanged a look of sudden complicity.

Twenty-six

Kevin walked nonchalantly into the shop. It took Margaret a moment to register surprise. At first, she simply felt glad to see him. Then, as she looked closely at his pale cheeks, she wondered if he too had a touch of 'flu.

'Margaret,' his voice was thin and anxious. 'I had no idea, no idea you were in danger.'

'Kevin,' she gasped, as if beginning the scene again. 'You're back.' She knew she should be angry with him, yet all she could feel was compassion for his drawn face and his troubled voice.

He claimed her hand. Uneasily she squeezed his palm. Now that the shock was wearing away, she felt a coldness between fear and fury.

'I thought if I left town, I . . . Well, to tell you the truth, it wasn't very smart. I thought Carson would feel easier with me out of the picture. I told him you wouldn't talk. I thought there was no way anyone could trace . . . I know, I know,' the words rushed like dry wind. 'I told him you knew nothing, none of the details.'

Gently she pulled back, folded her hands and asked, 'So why did you return? How?'

'You didn't know? Of course. Well, Chrissie found Mrs Hartley, who's retired to Monterey, and left a message that you had been threatened. Look, Margaret,' he sighed, 'you must think I'm despicable with the bribes and all. But they got out of hand. It was only supposed to happen once or twice. Christ, I never dreamed they would try to harm you.'

'I know,' she said heavily.

From behind, Margaret heard footsteps approaching the door. She kept her eyes on Kevin. Please God it wasn't Douglas. She could not bear his wrath. Dimly, she wondered at her inclination, after all this, to take care of Kevin. She could tell from the expression on his face that the person opening the door was not Douglas.

'Kevin!' Ernie was flabbergasted. 'Jesus, man, where the hell have you been? Do you know what . . .?'

'He knows,' Margaret cut him off.

'I came to turn myself in,' Kevin said slowly.

Margaret had an absurd memory of *Gunsmoke* and the surrender of honorable outlaws. Chrissie would say she was a damn fool, being so understanding and forgiving. However she had always known there was something confused about Kevin's involvement in this corruption. She was still angry, still incredulous, but with Kevin's appearance, she felt a small part of herself had been restored.

'Is Charles around the neighborhood?' Kevin asked.

'Charles?' Ernie was numb.

'I thought maybe you could take me down to the station.'

'Huh? Charles, no, he's out at San Francisco State this afternoon. Oh, what the fuck, no, it's his day off anyway.'

'I see,' Kevin looked around nervously, his attention drawn to the back of the shop.

'He's out,' Margaret explained. 'Should be back in fifteen minutes or so.'

'I was kind of hoping to avoid a reunion,' said Kevin.

'Here,' Ernie clapped Kevin's shoulder. 'I'll go down to the station with you.'

Kevin nodded gratefully.

Ernie couldn't meet his glance. He faced Margaret as he spoke, 'Let's leave now, I've got to get back to the stall soon.'

Chrissie hung up the phone and walked over to the couch by the window. She was too tired for the rocker this afternoon. Stretching out, she stared down at Geary Street, unable to focus on anything except Margaret's call about Kevin's surrender.

She knew it was only a matter of time until the headlines. Until the election. All this work telling people about their rights and Marissa would win because some con man screwed up! Chrissie closed her eyes, slid down on the couch and rested on the pillow Gudrun had crocheted for her last Christmas. The election didn't bear thinking about. Not just now. Marissa would win in four days time. That's what mattered, she tried to convince herself. That's all that mattered.

. . . James and Rajid kicking the soccer ball, calling her across the field. Exhausted after ten hours at Stuart's, she is suddenly rejuvenated as she runs toward . . .

Must have dropped off, Chrissie sat up. James and Rajid! She used to believe that dozing didn't happen to her, such a horse she was. Lately she had got slower. She'd never be able to kick that ball across the field now.

Startled by a shrieking siren, Chrissie looked down to find an ambulance buzzing like an impatient jigsaw through the Geary Street traffic.

Funny dream about James and Rajid. Douglas often reminded her of James. Douglas. No doubt Margaret would be comforting him now. They were probably commiserating, parent to parent. Children, such a burden, responsibility, legacy. And what kind of legacy would she leave? Who's to know she had been on earth? Who's to carry that wisdom, that look in the eye?

Chrissie stood and considered her image in the mirror. No one to carry it on. Maybe James's daughters. She truly must write to James's daughters. Checking the back of her hair in the hand mirror, she could see images in images. This was getting ridiculous. So much for afternoon naps.

Chrissie looked at her watch. An hour before work. She should go and talk to Douglas. However, she felt a little tired just now. Not tired enough to sleep. But too tired to navigate for a while yet.

Twenty-seven

CARSON ACCUSED OF FRAUD IN TOMORROW'S ELECTION
NEWS SHOP CLERK UNWITTING ACCOMPLICE

The newspapers were stacked high from the floor on Monday. Douglas, Margaret and Roberto stared at the headlines in a subdued haze.

'That one makes me look stupid,' Margaret said.

'Unwitting is different from witless,' answered Douglas, his attention drawn to another headline.

SEARCH OVER FOR MISSING MIDDLEMAN

'Missing middleman,' he repeated. 'If ever there was an apt description of my son.'

Margaret watched with concern.

'Don't give me one of your worried looks, Margaret. If you hadn't protected him in the first place . . .'

'No, that's not fair.' Roberto walked over to the older man and gripped his shoulder comfortingly.

'True,' said Douglas. 'I've never let that boy take responsibility for himself. That's why all this happened.'

Roberto shook his head. 'When do *you* grow up and stop being his father?'

'What do you think?' shot back Douglas. 'When are you going to let go of your daughters?'

'Douglas,' Margaret frowned, 'I didn't mean to hurt him.'

'No choice.' Douglas shook his head.

'And you *didn't* hurt him,' said Roberto. 'Typical, Mama. Typical, you being sorry for all this.'

She ignored Roberto. 'What will happen to him, Douglas?'

'When they try him — and I have no doubt they will — he'll be convicted and . . .' Douglas looked away, hiding from his own sudden tears.

'Oh, Douglas.' Margaret reached for his hand. Strong grip. White hairs. A little larger than Roger's hand.

176

'We'll celebrate,' Ernie spoke to Gudrun's smiling face. 'Two pecan pies à la mode. Oh,' he looked to Chrissie, 'will you indulge with us?'

'Are you joking?' asked Chrissie, unsure about the level of gruffness in her voice. She did mean to tease, but she was also annoyed. 'That would knock me out for the rest of the afternoon. Besides,' she shut her eyes, 'I won't celebrate anything until after the election tomorrow. Who knows what will happen next?'

'Kevin will descend in a white sheet sprinkled with gold glitter, announcing he's been born again,' Charles offered for Ernie's appreciation.

Chrissie exchanged a look of mock exasperation with Gudrun. Still, she found a smile escaping from her lips: 'Just coffee, love.'

'So how does it feel to be a regulation hero?' Ernie asked.

Chrissie wished she could gag the two of them and enjoy her break in peace. When she returned from holiday, she wouldn't tell anyone when her break was. She would spend it alone, maybe in the back alley, away from her friends and the Muzak and the aura of peppermint.

'Well, you had a certified murder threat.' Ernie stacked the menus neatly behind the pink plastic salt and pepper shakers. 'Threatened political assassination. Like Ronald Reagan. Gerald Ford.'

'Is he trying to insult me?' she asked Charles.

'I don't think it started out that way.'

'I'll tell you how I feel.' Chrissie craned her neck for Gudrun and the blessed coffee. 'Tired. Tired of all this nasty greed and dishonesty. Tired of struggling to elect someone to a job for which she's thoroughly qualified. Tired of working eight hours a day serving Blueberry Mountain Pancakes and Sunrise Omelettes. Ready to go to Hawaii and lie on the beach.'

Before she could finish, Gudrun appeared with two of the largest slices of pie Chrissie had ever seen pass across the floor of Mummer's. This woman must not care much about keeping her job.

'Swedish hospitality,' Ernie beamed at Gudrun. 'The Swedes are quite different from the Scots, as far as pie is concerned.'

'Thanks, Gudrun,' smiled Charles.

177

Chrissie wondered if he cared about Gudrun's crush on Ernie. Was Gudrun developing a crush on Charles, too? Oh, this woman. All of them! Chrissie had had enough of them all. She couldn't wait to get on that plane with Margaret.

'I'm fine now,' Margaret told Roger as he stared at her from the other end of the couch. 'And Marissa's won. That's the lasting effect of all this, the only thing that really matters now.'

'You could have told me about the bribes and the letter, Margaret.' He looked angry, no, more anxious, uncomprehending. He seemed paralyzed in his corner of the couch, his feet stiff on the broadloom as if secured by weights. 'You could have trusted me.' His voice shook.

'I know that.' Margaret took his hand, and in doing so, felt comfort. Her comforting him. She understood that it had always been this way. Even now he was asking why she hadn't discussed Kevin, not so much because he was upset about her welfare, but about her keeping secrets from him. She wished she could explain that she had always been afraid of what he would not say, just as she had been afraid of what Chrissie *would* say. She had wanted to avoid disappointment in him.

'I feel terrible you had to endure this alone.'

'Just for a while,' said Margaret.

'But you never talked to anyone.'

'I talked to Chrissie.'

'Oh, yes,' he sighed. 'Chrissie.' Then he adopted the solicitous ministering tone that was more familiar to Margaret. 'This must have been traumatic for both of you.'

'Yes.' Margaret was distant now, perhaps already in Hawaii. 'Hard. It's been hard.' The tears washed him into a blur. 'Hard,' she said as if the word itself were a sturdy bannister.

He moved closer on the couch. She knew he was going to tend to her. She tried to settle down and as he wrapped his arms around her, she willed herself to let go, to enjoy the momentary harbor.

'Oh, Margaret.' He had buried his head in her breasts and was crying. 'Margaret, Margaret,' he sobbed, 'it's not going to work, is it?'

Now she did relax, as if the candor had unsprung a stay in

178

the corset she thought she had discarded years ago. This relief admitted new sadness. Sadness that it hadn't succeeded with Roger, that once more she had lost the link. This love, which she had wanted so much, she could not want into being. She felt sorry for Roger. Sorry for his loss and his loneliness. She felt sorry for herself, but there was nothing she could do.

'No,' she said, careful not to leave him hanging, but she needn't have worried because he was weeping too loudly to hear.

Her own grief was profound. And solace would take some time. Chrissie would be no comfort. She had called Margaret a fool to get involved with him. Fool? Margaret didn't think so. She hurt; she was sad; but at least they had had a few weeks together. She knew that the vital parts of her were functioning. Holding Roger like this, she could feel the panic that hit when Bill left her. She remembered the desertion from when Janey moved to Canada. And she could almost sense the unbearable wrench from when Michael died. Loving had always hurt, yet it also kept a part of her, some fabric or tissue, alive.

'Are you sure?' he brushed away the tears with his fine, strong fingers, 'that we've given it enough time.'

'Yes,' she nodded sadly, 'enough.' She was surprised at this unequivocal clarity, but she had come to treasure time.

He kissed her hand and held it solemnly on his lap. Staring across the room, he seemed absorbed in the blank TV screen. Margaret closed her eyes until their silence was splintered by a blast of horns from the street below.

Twenty-eight

'I don't believe it,' Chrissie stared over Margaret's shoulder, across the airport.

Margaret shifted her small plaid suitcase and the pink overnight bag which Gudrun had lent her. She was aggravated with Chrissie for refusing to hire a porter. Aggravated with herself for giving in to Chrissie.

'Come on,' Margaret called. 'They've already announced the flight.' Such a seasoned tourist! First, Chrissie forgot her traveller's cheques and then she made them late to the airport.

'Relax. We're not boarding for twenty minutes. And look!'

Exasperated, Margaret set down her bags and turned around.

Blue balloons, a shower of confetti, three bottles of wine.

'Sneaky.' Ernie was running circles around them, sprinkling confetti. 'You two thought you'd escape the fanfare. Ve-ry sneaky.'

Charles sang, 'I left my heart in San Fran-cis-co.'

Was he high on something? considered Margaret. No, she could tell, just high on Ernie. Not a bad voice, but he might lower the volume. They were beginning to attract attention.

'Naughty,' Ernie said. 'Marissa is very irritated with you two, but she's got a meeting with the Mayor. And Roberto's taken Douglas out to visit Kevin in jail. You could have taught Howard Hughes a few lessons.'

Margaret grinned. She had agreed with Chrissie that they should make a quick escape. They had had enough excitement for one season. No need for elaborate goodbyes.

'So how did you two find out?' asked Chrissie. 'No, don't tell me. I don't want to hear about the TV monitors the police have hidden in my apartment.'

'Don't blame me,' said Charles. 'An ex-policeman can't be held accountable.'

'Are you serious about the TV monitors?' fretted Margaret, who had by now completely forgotten about the airplane.

Ernie hugged her and shook his head.

'Ex-policeman?' asked Chrissie.

'He's talked me back to school,' said Charles. 'Community planning at State.'

'Well, good for you,' said Margaret.

'Yes,' nodded Chrissie. 'Marissa,' she asked, 'is not really mad, is she?'

'Sure she is,' said Ernie. 'She wanted to say goodbye, but she's also pretty resigned to you. All she said was, "Well, I should have expected it . . ." '

'Flight 415 for Honolulu is now boarding.'

Margaret glared at Chrissie.

Before Chrissie could respond, Ernie and Charles swooped up their bags, moved between the women and linked arms with them.

At the gate, Margaret flapped nervously for her ticket. And her address book. And her wallet.

'Anyone would think you didn't want to make this trip,' said Chrissie.

'Oh, hush. I just wanted to make sure everything is in order.'

'Never,' laughed Ernie, 'will everything be in order.'

'I'm beginning to understand that,' said Margaret.

Arguing behind them. Man and a woman. The four friends turned to find an Indian couple whispering heatedly.

'This is the wrong queue,' he said.

'No, the right one,' she said. 'I'm certain of it.'

Chrissie had noticed the charter to India. A distant gate. Why had she noticed it? She started to direct them when the man said to her, 'Is this the flight to Honolulu?'

Chrissie was too surprised to answer. Margaret interceded, 'Yes, this is the right gate.' She added confidently, 'Boarding now.'

The line moved quickly. Ernie and Charles returned their bags.

'See you in two weeks,' Ernie said. 'Four pm. I've checked your return flight with our friendly travel agent.'

'Och, get on with you,' Chrissie said.

'No,' Ernie pointed to the line accelerating toward the gate, 'get on with *you*.'

181

Once Margaret had a couple of sips from her daiquiri, she was fine. Chrissie had been studying the paper intently, ignoring takeoff procedures and emergency exit locations. Margaret, who had listened carefully to all the steward's instructions, was now relaxed enough to sit back and enjoy the view. Flying above the clouds. She thought she'd never experience this until she was dead. Maybe she was dead, on her way to heaven. In heaven. After all, she was holding her daiquiri and Chrissie was right beside her. She looked over Chrissie's shoulder and saw yet more stories about the election.

She thought back on Marissa's victory party at Glide. Music and dancing and shouting and speechmaking. Even more excitement than that night she had attended the rally with Chrissie. At first, the victory celebration had seemed alien — filled with loud, hearty political people. As she began to relax, she recognized the revellers. Ernie dancing the twist with Gudrun in her tight turquoise dress. That woman never gave up! Charles and Roberto conspiring quietly. Chrissie arguing with Gus and Harvey about pension legislation. Marissa listening intently to five people talking at once, her face tired and her eyes wide awake. After Margaret slipped into the noise and excitement, she didn't feel so foreign. At one point, Chrissie interrupted a strategic argument and turned to her, saying, 'You all right?' Margaret hadn't been sure if this was a question or a command, but she nodded yes.

Now, as Chrissie flipped to the next section of *The Chronicle*, she handed the other to Margaret. To avoid argument, Margaret accepted the newspaper and held it on her lap. She had no more heart for reading. She knew all she needed about Carson. Kevin had been only one of four people filtering him money from real estate interests. However, aside from Carson himself, Kevin was the single arrest. And so he was implicated in the campaign violence. Margaret remembered now, Kevin pale and frightened the day she visited him in jail. Douglas exhausted, bedridden for a week after his son's surrender. She and Douglas unable to communicate. The two of them sick and dumb and confined. 'Mrs Hartley,' Margaret said spontaneously, recalling the woman waiting to see Kevin after her visit.

'Yes, Mrs Hartley,' Chrissie repeated, studying Margaret

over her reading glasses. 'You've told me, hen. Mrs Hartley was *sick*. Kevin *was* telling the truth about *that*.' Provoked, she demanded, 'What does it mean? Does it erase the bribery and the lies? Listen, he was lucky that plea bargaining got him a light sentence.'

'Oh, go back to,' Margaret peered over Chrissie's shoulder, 'back to BOMBINGS IN BEIRUT.''

Margaret recalled Ernie's reassurances about Kevin, that they would give him some kind of safe office work. But Margaret had heard San Bruno was a dangerous place.

Chrissie worried about Margaret's continuing depression. She had almost refused to take this trip because of Kevin. Angel of Lost Causes. Truth was, Chrissie felt sorry for him now that the election was settled. He had truly been a pawn — lying and dangerous all right, but a pawn.

Lately Chrissie was startled at her own compassion. She had actually felt bad for Roger Bentman when he took off to that ecumenical convention in Boston. So tired and defeated he looked getting into the taxi. Well, enough of that, Margaret was the one she should cheer up.

Chrissie pulled out a brochure about their hotel. Margaret turned back from the window.

'Swimming, miniature golf,' Chrissie recited. 'And we can take a ride up to the volcanoes.'

'I'm not that keen on outdoor vigor,' Margaret grimaced. 'I thought we were going for a rest.'

'Definitely.' Chrissie had half-listened. 'Plenty of sleep. And I've got a letter here from a woman named Miriam Schwam. She's a Gray Panther in Honolulu and she said she wants us to speak.'

'Us?' exclaimed Margaret.

'About the situation for senior citizens in San Francisco.'

'Us?'

'And,' Chrissie ignored her, 'there's a local election rally, a benefit.'

'You're kidding,' Margaret interrupted, then saw that Chrissie was not kidding.

'They thought we might be useful.'

'We?' asked Margaret. However, Chrissie was not listening. Margaret sipped her daiquiri and looked out over the clouds.

She was going to Hawaii, she told herself. She was going to Hawaii with Chrissie.